BiGGER than a Bread Box

Bigger than a Bread Box

LAUREL SNYDER

Random House 🏠 New York

Text copyright © 2011 by Laurel Snyder
Jacket art copyright © 2011 by Steve James

Grateful acknowledgment is made to the following for permission
to reprint previously published material:

Grubman Indursky & Shire, P.C.: Excerpt from "Hungry Heart" by Bruce Springsteen, copyright
© 1980 by Bruce Springsteen (ASCAP). All rights reserved. International copyright secured.
Reprinted by permission of Grubman Indursky & Shire, P.C.

Northwestern University Press and William Meredith: "The Illiterate" by William Meredith,
copyright © 1997 by William Meredith. Originally published by TriQuarterly Books/Northwestern
University Press. All rights reserved. Reprinted by permission of Northwestern University Press
and William Meredith.

All rights reserved. Published in the United States by Random House Children's Books,
a division of Random House, Inc., New York.

Random House and the colophon are registered trademarks of Random House, Inc.

Visit us on the Web!
www.randomhouse.com/kids

Educators and librarians, for a variety of teaching tools,
visit us at www.randomhouse.com/teachers

Library of Congress Cataloging-in-Publication Data
Snyder, Laurel.
Bigger than a bread box / by Laurel Snyder. — 1st ed.
p. cm.
Summary: Devastated when her parents separate, twelve-year-old Rebecca must move with her
mother from Baltimore to Gran's house in Atlanta, where Rebecca discovers an old bread box with
the power to grant any wish—so long as the wished-for thing fits in the bread box.
ISBN 978-0-375-86916-7 (trade) — ISBN 978-0-375-96916-4 (lib. bdg.) —
ISBN 978-0-375-89998-0 (ebook)
[1. Wishes—Fiction. 2. Divorce—Fiction. 3. Moving, Household—Fiction.
4. Homesickness—Fiction.] I. Title.
PZ7.S6851764Bi 2011   [Fic]—dc22   2010047307

Printed in the United States of America
10 9 8 7 6 5 4 3 2 1
First Edition

Random House Children's Books supports
the First Amendment and celebrates the right to read.

For Mom, Dad, and Baltimore.

My homes.

BiGGER than a Bread Box

Before

I remember this one time: Mary Kate and I were at the playground, sitting in the swings, waiting for Mr. Softee to make his way down the hill to us. We could hear the tinkling music from his truck, and I had a sweaty five-dollar bill crumpled in my fist. My feet were dirty in their yellow flip-flops. It was summer.

Then, right in front of our faces, a seagull swooped down out of nowhere and landed a few feet away, by the rusty slide. The bird wasn't scared of us at all. It had half a ham sandwich in its mouth.

Mary Kate kicked in the direction of the gull and said, "Ugh, seagulls. They're so gross."

The bird didn't move.

I kicked too. "Yeah, gross."

Mary Kate was right. Seagulls *are* gross. They scream at you and poop on your head. They eat garbage. They have ugly feet and angry eyes. They like meat and they're always hungry. Only people who don't know seagulls think they're perfect and pretty—all white and soaring and dipping and everything.

But I was kind of impressed with this seagull. He didn't care that we were bigger than him. He didn't care that we were kicking at him. He didn't even move when we got up and ran right past him to buy our ice cream. That seagull had a sandwich and he was going to eat it. It was his playground and he wasn't going anywhere.

I never forgot that dumb bird.

CHAPTER 1

I was in the dining room part of the kitchen doing my math homework at the table when the lights suddenly blinked off. Everything else in the house stopped working too. The numbers on the microwave's clock disappeared. The fridge stopped making the wheezy noise it usually makes.

Then my mom, over in the living room, started picking on my dad for no good reason. As far as I could tell, he was just sitting on the couch, drinking a beer and watching TV, like he usually does after dinner. "Winding down," he calls it. Ever since he wrecked his cab, he's been winding down a lot. But the accident wasn't his fault, and he'll get another job soon. He always does. He's just taking a break for a little while.

Anyway, I couldn't see either of them because of the lights being off, but I could hear everything they said. There weren't doors or walls between the downstairs rooms in our row house. The flooring just changed color every ten feet or so. You knew you were out of the kitchen/dining room and into the living room when the fake-brick linoleum stopped and the pale blue carpet started. Then you were out of the living room and into the front room when the blue carpet changed to brown. That was how a lot of row houses were in Baltimore, like tunnels.

So, really, we were all in one long, dark room together when Mom snapped, "Jim! You didn't pay the power bill again?"

Dad didn't answer her. He does that sometimes, tunes out, though I can never tell if he's daydreaming or just pretending not to hear her. She kept going on about how she was "sick of it all." She said she was too tired to even talk about it anymore, but then she kept talking. She called him selfish. She said he was a child. She went on and on, and none of it made much sense to me. It was just a big list of angry. Her voice got madder and louder until at last she was yelling when she said, "If you can't handle the bills right now, could you maybe at least handle the dishes?"

Even though it was pitch-black in the room, I squeezed my eyes shut. I laid my head on the table, on my math book.

She stopped yelling and got quiet. Everything was dark and quiet when she said, in a smaller voice, "I'm sorry, Jim," and "I hate this," and "I love you, but . . ."

I squeezed my eyes tighter.

Then Mom started crying.

I just sat in the dark dining area with my head on my book. Partly because I absolutely didn't want to go in *there,* but also partly because it was so dark I was afraid I'd trip over a chair or something. I just sat, hunched over. I smelled the musty paper of the math book and listened to Mom cry. It was hardly the first time they'd had a fight in front of me, but things didn't usually get so bad.

After a while, Mom stopped and kind of whispered, "You know, Jim? I could do this . . . just as easily . . . without you."

There was a pause after that; then Dad said, really, really softly, "Oh . . . *could* you?"

Mom sucked in a quick breath, like it hurt her, and she said, "Yeah. Easier even."

Dad sat there, I guess, doing nothing. That was what it sounded like. It sounded like nothing.

Mom took another breath, a slow one this time, and asked, "Did you hear what I said? Did you hear me? Aren't you going to say *anything?*"

I opened my eyes. She sounded calm, too calm. Something was really wrong.

Dad, not yelling or crying—because he pretty much never yells or cries—said, "What do you want me to say, Annie?" He sounded grim. He was talking through his teeth. I heard him take a big wet sip of his beer before he said, "You think I like the way things are any better than you?"

She didn't answer him.

I couldn't stand it after that. It was totally dark and quiet. I'd never been anywhere so still as that room. It was like I was waiting in the back of a closet, sitting on lumpy shoes. Only there was no door to open, nothing I could do to get out. I'd never listened so carefully to something I didn't want to hear.

Then two things happened at the same exact time.

The lights came back on.

And upstairs, in his room, my little brother, Lew, started crying.

"Mama?" he was saying. "Daddy?"

I looked over into the living room. With the lights back on, I could see everything clearly again. My parents were just frozen there, like statues. Lew kept crying.

I stood up. I made myself walk. I kept my eyes on my feet. Even so, out of the corner of my eye I could see Mom leaning against the side of the recliner, still wearing her blue scrubs from work, her arms limp and her face all wet. Dad was sitting on the couch, staring past her at the blank TV. He looked sad too, but also, weirdly, he looked a little like he wanted to smile. I guess maybe that was because now everyone knew he *had* paid the power bill.

I didn't say anything to either of them, and they didn't say anything to me. I walked as fast as I could through the living room and headed up the stairs to Lew. Poor kid. He wasn't even three years old yet. He had no idea what was going on.

When I got upstairs, Lew was in his crib, holding the bars really tight. His face was red, but when he saw me, he stopped crying. I lifted him out. He can climb out himself, but he doesn't usually do it. We sat on the floor, and I held him and rocked while he sucked his thumb. He smelled like dirty hair and peanut butter. I thought about singing a song but didn't. Eventually, he fell back asleep in my lap, and I laid him on the floor, because I knew I'd wake him up putting him into his crib. My arms aren't long enough, so I always have to drop him the last foot, deadweight, and he wakes up. Instead I just covered him with a blanket.

That was near the end of October.

CHAPTER 2

On Halloween, for the first time ever, Dad and I stayed home with the bowl of candy on the porch, eating all the peanut butter cups ourselves, while Mom took Lew trick-or-treating. Lew dressed up as a last-minute ghost, even though he'd asked to be a pirate. I watched him walk off down the street, a little blob of white holding Mom's hand and a plastic orange pumpkin. It felt weird, lonely, watching the two of them walk off down the hill without us.

But, for the most part, I couldn't see that anything had really changed after the fight, except that Dad slept on the couch. Mom had asked him to go and stay somewhere else for a while, but he said it was his house too, and he wasn't going to be put out of it.

What I hated most was having to say good night twice. First to Dad on the couch, in the dark with the TV turned down low, then to Mom in her bed with a book in her hand. During the day, there was a big pile of blankets that stayed on the couch, and that was pretty fun. When I came home from school in the afternoons, Mary Kate and I would make a big nest out of the blankets and watch TV and eat ramen with extra soy sauce. We would practice using chopsticks, and we'd eat and spill and watch shows we weren't supposed to watch. I hoped that when Mom decided to stop being mad, and she and Dad worked things out, we could keep the pile of blankets downstairs.

I was beginning to think that everything was about to blow over. Then, one cold Wednesday morning, I came downstairs for breakfast and found that Mom had all our mismatched suitcases laid out on the floor in the living room.

"Where are you going?" I asked her.

"*We're* going on a trip," she said.

"What about school?" I asked. "It's Wednesday."

"You can miss some school this once," she said, pulling an old sock from the bottom of a backpack. I wondered how long the sock had been in there. We didn't take trips very often. Almost never.

"Okay . . . I guess," I said. "Only where are we going?"

"Home," she answered softly. "We're going home."

"Oh."

I knew that by "home" she meant Atlanta, and Gran. That was the only place besides Baltimore she could possibly mean when she said "home." It was where Mom was from, where she'd grown up. Gran usually flew up to see us for Christmas, though Dad made a point of calling those visits "Hanukkah vacation." He wasn't very Jewish, my dad, but Christmas always made him grumpy.

We hadn't been to Atlanta to see Gran in years. Mom was always saying we'd go next year, but when "next year" came, she never seemed to have the time off for a vacation. I tried to remember Gran's house, but all I could picture was a lot of dark wood trim, purple curtains, and a yard full of flowers.

"Dad too?" I asked, even though I was pretty sure I knew the answer.

Mom didn't say anything.

"When will we come back?" I asked after a minute.

She fidgeted with a broken zipper on a green duffel bag. "As soon as I feel like it makes sense to."

I went to get some breakfast, like any other day.

Lew was at the table, putting dry Cheerios into a spoon with his fingers. He usually eats like that, fills his fork or his spoon with his fingers. He drops a lot on the floor, so it takes a while. When he has the spoon full, he puts it in his mouth.

I could see Dad through the cutout window separating the eating part of the kitchen from the cooking part. The window is there because once upon a time, before we lived there, the cooking part of the room was the back porch. Now we don't have a back porch, just three steps that drop down into our skinny little backyard.

Dad was standing at the sink with a coffee filter over one hand, staring off into space. He was like a statue of a guy making coffee, except that his hands were shaking. His mouth was a thin straight line, tight, like someone had sewn it shut.

"Hi, Dad," I said, walking around to him and taking a banana from the bowl beside him on the counter. It didn't feel like the right thing to say, but I couldn't think of anything else.

"Hi, Becks." His voice sounded like he had a sore throat.

I went back to the table and sat down next to Lew. Dad didn't follow me; he just stood beside the sink, looking at me and Lew. Then he stared past us, at Mom and the suitcases, two rooms away.

I willed him to say something else, to stop what was happening. I tried to send him a psychic message. I peeled my banana very carefully and ate it as slowly as I could, to give him a chance to step in and fix things, but I guess he didn't get the message.

I don't know what happened after I went to the bus stop, but when I got home from school that day, the car was packed. I didn't get to pick out my own stuff. I didn't get to say goodbye to Mary Kate, who had stayed home from school because she was sick. I didn't even get to tell her we were leaving.

Mom was waiting on the porch with Lew. Dad was standing down in the street, by our old green car, looking like he might throw up. His hand was on the roof of the car. I went over and stood beside him.

Mom started down the steps, dragging Lew along with her. When she got to the sidewalk, she let go of his hand and took out her keys. She seemed to be in a big hurry.

"Annie, don't," Dad said to her. He scraped a fingernail across the flaking paint on top of the car. Then he put his hands in his pockets. "Please, *don't.*"

I thought maybe he would try grabbing her or hugging her or kneeling or something, like in a movie. He didn't.

Mom lifted Lew into his car seat in the back. She snapped him in and shut the door. "Get in, Rebecca!" she said, opening her own door and motioning to the passenger seat beside her. She slid in and stuck the key into the ignition.

I stood there on the sidewalk, looking back and forth from my mom in the car to my dad beside me on the pavement. I remember it was really windy. Cold for fall. The sky was pale gray, almost white, like it is sometimes over the harbor. A gull screamed.

"Say goodbye, Rebecca," said my mom.

"But—"

"It's time to go," she snapped. Then she closed her eyes and took a deep breath. She let it out. "Don't worry, you'll see your father again. This isn't the end of the world."

She was wrong. It *was* the end of the world. Everything felt wrong, lopsided. I knew from the weird fuzzy humming inside my head.

Lew smiled and waved. "Bye, Daddy." He thought we were running errands or something—going to the Safeway maybe.

My dad opened his mouth, but no words came out. His hands were in his jeans pockets. His shoulders were hunched, but he still wasn't saying or doing anything.

I looked at him and I looked at him, and he looked different than he'd ever looked to me before. Thinner. He wasn't wearing a coat. I memorized him. My heart felt cold in my chest, but I didn't know what to say or do either.

At last I kind of fell into him. I rubbed my face against his soft flannel shirt. A button scraped my cheek.

Then he took his hands out of his pockets and bent over me, to hug me. I put my arms around his chest. He didn't make a sound, and there were no tears, but his body was shaking all around me, like a silent movie of someone crying. Or maybe he was just shivering in the wind. He smelled a little like cigarette smoke and a lot like sweat. My dad. My dad. My dad was so strong. He *never* cried. "I don't know . . . ," he whispered to me. Answering a question I hadn't asked.

I felt frozen. Stuck to him, stuck *with* him in a bubble, in that hug so tight it was bruising my arms. We were going to leave *him*—my dad—and there was nothing I could do. It wasn't possible. It was too fast. I just hugged and hugged and hugged.

But then.

Then my mother, behind me, said in a tiny voice, "Rebecca, please? Don't make this any harder for me."

And I listened.

I didn't have to listen. I shouldn't have, but I did. I turned my head from my dad and unhugged him. I pulled away from his arms, wiggled out, opened the car door, and ducked inside. I looked at my lap. I didn't look at him. If he wasn't going to cry, then I wasn't going to cry either. I could be strong too.

Dad followed, leaned in after me through the open door, grabbed my chin with his cold hand, and turned my face toward him. He kissed me on the forehead. He put something in my hand, folded my fingers shut, and squeezed my fist with his own big hand. "I love you," he said. "I love you, Becks. So much love."

Which was funny to hear out loud. He didn't say things like that very often.

He reached back to touch Lew, but just then my mom turned the key, started the engine. The car made a big noise. My door was still open.

Over the noise of the car, through my open door, Dad said, "Annie, please? We can still . . . They're my kids. . . . I'll try to . . . Don't *do* this. . . ."

"I already did," she said. "We'll call you when we get there."

That was how we left him, through an open car door. My mom stepped on the gas. The car began to move. My dad jumped back to the sidewalk, off balance. When I turned around, I could see him standing in the street. He was calling after us. My *dad* was yelling in the street for everyone to hear; then he was running behind the car. He was calling, "Come back! Come back!"

I whipped back around to make sure Mom was seeing that, to make sure she had seen Dad yelling and running after us. But I guess she didn't care, because she turned a corner, and we were gone. The open car door scraped the ground for a full block before I finally managed to pull it shut. The sound was terrible, grinding.

I put on my seat belt. What else could I do?

"Daddy?" Lew said, trying to turn around in his car seat. "Daddy?"

Nobody answered him, so he put his stinky blue blanket over his head and slurped his thumb.

We drove for a while like that. Mom turned on the radio to a news show full of serious voices talking about hurricane refugees. Under his blanket, Lew fell asleep like he always does on the highway.

After a minute, I opened my fingers to see what the cold thing in my hand was, to see what my dad had given me. It was a necklace, Grandma Shapiro's white gold locket, the one she was wearing in the picture on the living room wall, beside the other old black-and-white pictures of people I didn't know. We didn't visit much with our out-of-town family, and I didn't remember ever meeting my father's mother. There were only a few pictures in our photo albums, of me in her lap, and then of me and Dad at her funeral. I remembered Dad saying she'd died in that locket.

Dad didn't talk much to his family. They mostly lived far away, in Florida. Occasionally we got cards from them, for Jewish holidays and birthdays, with pictures of college-age cousins whose names I could barely remember. Dad didn't even go to family weddings. He didn't like fuss, he said, any more than he liked Florida. Mom said at least Dad *had* a family.

I opened the locket with a fingernail and stared at the picture inside, a tiny photo of my dad as a baby, a little circle of faded color. He looked like Lew, with his hair in soft brown wings on either side of his round face. I closed the locket again and fastened it around my neck. It felt cold and smooth against my skin, and heavier than I'd expected.

I tried to remember the last time my dad had given me something, and I couldn't. But Dad didn't have to give presents or say special words, because there were all these little things about him. Like how he slapped his chest with his hands in the morning while he sang "You Are My Sunshine." How he put extra butter on the popcorn when Mom wasn't looking. How he got really happy watching old black-and-white movies about manly men and pretty ladies. I didn't watch movies like that by myself, but I loved them on Sunday afternoon with Dad. I thought about how he looked serious when he lit candles on Friday night, which was really the only Jewish thing he ever did. Whenever Mom was gone at dinnertime, Dad made scrambled eggs with cheese.

It made me sad, thinking so much about him, even though the memories were happy, so I decided to stop. Instead I stared out the window and watched the trees go past. I remember thinking that I was riding in the front seat for the first time ever on a long trip. It was a weird thing to be thinking, but I couldn't help it. Usually I was stuck in the back with Lew drooling beside me or—if he was awake—flinging raisins and animal crackers at my head. Now, up front, I could see ahead. I could see everything for myself.

I watched the road without saying anything to my mom. Periodically she would point to some bird flying by or something, and sigh. I knew she wanted me to notice, to sigh with her, so that we could start chatting and then talk about things. But I wasn't going to give her the satisfaction. Mom always wanted to talk about things, about every last little detail of her life. I knew that talking would make her feel better, and that it would probably make me feel worse.

After about a half hour, she picked up her phone with her right hand and, with her left hand still on the wheel, dialed. I guess Gran didn't pick up because Mom left a message. "We're on our way" was all she said, which meant Gran was expecting us.

I really didn't want to break the silence, so I just sat there and said nothing, until, as we flew past the WELCOME TO VIRGINIA sign, I couldn't hold it any longer.

"I have to pee," I said.

Mom sighed and kept driving.

"I have to pee *bad*."

Finally she said, "Oh, Rebecca, I'm so, so sorry," in a shaky voice.

"I just have to pee is all," I mumbled, not looking at her.

It was really late when we got to Atlanta. I was asleep, but I remember Mom poking my shoulder and saying softly, "We're here, honey." I opened my eyes. The car was parked beside a big hedge with flowers on it. Flowers in November? When I opened my door, I could smell them: too sweet, like old lady perfume. There was a streetlight shining down yellow.

We climbed out of the car into what felt like spring, and Mom carried Lew up a set of brick steps while I followed behind her. The door swung open, and Gran was standing there in a nightgown and robe, looking sad and happy at the same time, with her short gray hair sticking straight up in the air. She hugged me. When she let go, she pointed me down a long central hallway full of doors and dark wood trim—just like I remembered—toward a pink door. I felt funny, like I was sleepwalking. I walked down the hall and pushed open the door. I pulled off my shoes and socks and jeans. I crawled into bed in my T-shirt and underpants. Almost instantly, I fell back asleep.

Chapter 3

I woke up in the morning in a strange bed in a strange room. Gran's house smelled like coffee and bacon, and there was too much sun in my eyes. I climbed down from the bed and looked out a big window at the leaves still green on the tree beside the house. Through the leaves, I could see a flat blue sky, an empty sky. It took me a second to realize why that was weird.

No gulls? I looked in every direction, but I didn't see a single bird. A city without seagulls? It seemed wrong. It had never occurred to me that there weren't gulls everywhere.

I put on my jeans from the day before. I felt at my neck to make sure the locket was still there. Then I looked around. I could tell right away that the room had been my mother's when she was a kid. I had a faint sense of having been in it before. There were pictures of her on the desk, all of them very smiley, and there was a plaque with her name on it. She'd won second place for archery. Archery? *Really?* The wallpaper was a pattern of faded flowers, and the bedspread and curtains were as pink as the door. I didn't like pink. I liked blue. There were old dolls on a high shelf. There was a bookcase full of paperback books, mysteries mostly, as if my mom had left that room when she was a teenager and nobody had been in it since then. Though I knew that wasn't true.

I opened the pink door.

From the hallway, I could hear Mom and Lew and Gran eating breakfast and talking loudly. I followed the sound and listened. Gran was fussing over Lew. She was saying, "Here's a bitty bite for a hungry boy." I guess she was trying to feed him, even though he was too old for that, but when I stepped into the doorway, I saw he was smiling and getting all sticky with syrup. He seemed to be enjoying the fuss as much as the pancakes.

Everyone looked up at me and stopped what they were doing, like they'd all been waiting for me.

Lew smiled and waved. "Babecka!"

Mom set down her coffee and said, "Hey, sleepyhead."

I shot her what I hoped was a mean look and didn't say anything back.

Gran threw open her arms and shouted, "Rebecca! Let me look at you! You've gotten so big!"

I hugged her, of course, because even when you're

being mad, you can't *not* hug the grandmother you haven't seen for almost a year. I was glad to see her, and to prove it, I let her make me a plate of pancakes and bacon, and then I ate until I felt too full. Grandmothers like to see you eat too much. Besides, we never had bacon at home. Dad didn't keep kosher or anything, but for some reason he hated bacon. Too bad for him, because bacon is delicious, especially when it just happens to bump into some pancake syrup.

Once I was finished, I set down my fork and turned to my mom. "*Now* what?"

"Well," she said with a forced smile, pretending it wasn't the first thing I'd said to her since we'd stopped to pee in Virginia the day before. "It's been so long since we were last here, Gran and I were thinking we'd have a fun day today. See the sights! Since it's a nice morning, we thought we might walk to the zoo. I always loved the zoo." Mom sat there, waiting for me to be excited. She was still grinning, but her eyes looked tired and red.

I made her wait a little longer before I said, "No, *now what*? What are we doing here? How long are we staying? I didn't even say goodbye to Mary Kate. I need to call her."

"Annie!" Gran cried, whipping around to stare at my mom. "You didn't *tell* them? You didn't explain?"

"There wasn't time," said my mom, looking down at her plate.

"Explain what?" I asked.

"It's a twelve-hour drive from Maryland to Georgia," said Gran. "How long does it take?"

"Tell us what?" I asked, remembering that long, silent ride.

"It didn't feel like the right time," mumbled my mother.

Gran made a disappointed face at my mom. Then she turned to me and Lew and said, "You're all going to stay here with me for a while."

"But . . . what about school?"

"You'll go to school here, in Atlanta. Just for a bit. Until your mom and dad can get everything all sorted out. Okay? There's a great middle school just a few streets over, where I used to sometimes volunteer in the library. It's a wonderful place. My friend Judy is a secretary there, and she's already processed all the paperwork so they can let you in midyear. Isn't that nice? Lew can hang out with me during the day. I've been looking forward to it! Retirement is boring." She made a face at Lew, who wasn't saying a word. He was just watching the rest of us carefully.

"What!" I yelled, flipping around to my mom. "You found me a school? You said we were going on a trip. A trip is like a week, maybe."

"I said we'd go home when it made sense to, and we will, but nothing makes sense right now. And when I called Gran to talk, she offered—"

"You didn't say we were *moving*."

"We aren't. Not permanently, I don't think, and anyway,

I didn't know," said my mom, looking into my eyes. "I wasn't sure. I'm still not. About anything."

I turned away from her again. "I hate you," I whispered. "I hate you."

"I know," she said in a deflated way.

I didn't feel sorry for her. It was one thing to *run* away. People got mad and ran away from things all the time, but then they cooled down. It was something else to *stay* away.

Mom reached for my shoulder. "Please understand, Rebecca," she said. "I need some time to think, some headspace. I need help. I have a lot to figure out, and it's nice for me . . . to be home, with Gran. Plus, I was able to set things up so that I can take shifts at a hospital here. It'll only take a week or two to get my license in Georgia, so I can keep the bills paid in Baltimore while I get my head together."

"You got a job here?"

"Well, not a permanent job or anything. I'll just pick up extra shifts when I can. I'll just be what they call a traveling nurse. Please . . . try to understand. . . ."

"It's November," I said, turning back around to face her, suddenly feeling like I couldn't breathe. "It's the middle of the year. I don't know anybody here. I won't have any friends."

"You will, Rebecca," said my mom softly. "You'll make friends. I promise."

"But . . . Dad—"

"Your dad'll be just fine. He'll make it work. And I promise, you'll get to see him."

"How can you know he'll be fine?" I asked. "How can you do this?" I stood up and my chair fell behind me with a bang, but I didn't pick it up. I just ran out of the kitchen.

Mom called out, "Please . . . come back and let's talk about this!"

In the hall, I flattened my back against the wall so nobody could see me standing there from the kitchen. I had no idea what to do and I didn't know where to go, but I couldn't be in the same room with her. I couldn't stand her face. We *weren't* going to talk about it. I was never talking to her again, ever.

"Rebecca!" I heard Gran call loudly.

They probably thought I was off sobbing on that awful pink bed, but I wasn't going to cry.

Mom said to Gran, "Let her go. It's a shock. This is going to be hard. She probably needs to be mad at me right now."

I did. I *was* mad, and it only made me madder to listen to her trying to sound all understanding and loving and motherly when she was anything but. Still, I listened from the hall. I wanted to know what they were saying.

"I can't believe you didn't explain this to her, Annie," said Gran. "She's not a little girl. She's twelve. Almost a teenager. What were you thinking?"

"I guess I *wasn't* thinking," I heard my mother say.

I wanted to call my dad. I'd ask him to come and get me, ask him to bring me back home with him, and Lew too. Mom could stay here and "rest up" by herself. She could "rest up" all she needed just fine without us! She could see how it felt to be alone. How *Dad* felt.

Unfortunately, I didn't know where the phone was in this house. I didn't know where anything was. Quietly I stepped away from the wall and tiptoed down the hallway, in search of a phone.

The first door I opened was a pink-tiled bathroom. Ugh, more pink.

The second door was a closet that smelled like mothballs. Everything inside it was covered with plastic bags.

The third door led to what looked like Gran's room, and lots of plaid.

Behind the fourth door was a steep, narrow staircase. I climbed the stairs, my hands touching the walls on either side of me. There wasn't a railing.

At the top of the stairs was a dusty attic. "Clutter" was the word that jumped into my head when I saw it. Light streamed in from two dirty windows at either end of the big slanty-roofed room, onto piles of dusty boxes and pieces of forgotten furniture: a broken rocking chair, an old sewing machine attached to a table, a light blue kitchen chair. I was pretty sure I wouldn't find a phone up there, but I couldn't help poking around anyway. It was interesting. We didn't have an attic in Baltimore. When things took up too much space, we had a yard sale.

In one corner a plastic Christmas tree gathered dust. The lights were wired onto the branches, and old threads of silver tinsel clung to the needles. One old candy cane hung from a spindly branch. Next to the tree was an old metal washtub full of moth-eaten linens and a wooden ironing board. Beside that was a box labeled ANNIE'S THINGS.

Along the sloping wall behind the washtub was a set of low shelves with a bunch of old boxes. They were all different. Some were metal, and some were wood. Some were painted bright colors, and some were falling apart. I could tell they were bread boxes because most of them were painted or stamped with the word "Bread." I guess it was a collection, but it seemed weird to go to the trouble of collecting a bunch of stuff and then just stick it all in an attic.

I began opening the boxes. Some were rusted shut, and I had to really work to pry them open, but except for a few dead bugs and a lot of dust, each box I opened was empty. I lost interest and sat down in the tub of dingy linens. It was comfortable, and I decided not to go back downstairs for a while. Let them wonder where I was!

I sat like that and thought about how Dad would come and rescue me. I made it into a little movie in my head. I pictured him driving up to the house. I pictured myself carrying Lew down the steps. I pictured Mom, wringing her hands on the steps, calling after us. I pictured us driving away.

Then it occurred to me that we'd taken the car when we left, so with his cab totaled, there was no way for Dad to drive anywhere. The movie in my head faded, and I sneezed from the dust.

I wondered how long it would be before someone found me in the attic. Eventually either Mom or Gran was sure to come looking. I wouldn't need to eat for hours, after all those pancakes, but how long could I last in a dirty attic with nothing to do? I wished I'd grabbed one of the paperbacks from the bookshelf in the room downstairs.

"What am I going to do with myself up here?" I asked a scratched oil painting of a girl sitting on a footstool in an old-fashioned red dress, holding a book. A little brass plate on the frame read "Molly Moran."

"I wish *I* had a book," I said to Molly.

Molly stared back at me, with eyes so dark they were almost black. Her face was pale and thin, framed by brown curls. She looked sad. But of course she didn't answer me, so I got out of the washtub and pawed around in the boxes some more, looking for anything that might keep me busy. Maybe I'd come across an old puzzle, a pad of paper and a pencil, anything. It seemed strange that with all the other junk in the attic, there weren't any books, or even a stack of old *National Geographic*s.

I found some dishes and more clothes. On every

windowsill, and attached to the underside of most of the furniture, I found soft white spider eggs.

Finally, after I'd looked through each box and bucket in that dirty, dusty attic, I came back to the bread boxes. There were only three I hadn't looked inside of yet, and I opened them now. The first two, a plain tin box and a rusted yellow box, were empty. Then I reached for the door of the last box, a red one with roses painted on it. On the lid, a flowery cursive read, "Give Us This Day Our Daily Bread." As bread boxes went, it was pretty nice. The door opened smoothly.

And inside it was a book! I took it out and shut the box with a smooth click.

The book in my hand was hardly one I'd have chosen if I'd been at the library, where I usually spent Saturday mornings with Mary Kate, but it was something to read. It was called *The Secret Adversary,* by Agatha Christie. The cover was falling apart.

I settled back down into the tub of linens and got lost reading.

I didn't notice when the door at the bottom of the stairs opened. I didn't notice anyone on the steps. I didn't notice anything until Gran was standing above me, flicking a switch. The attic flooded with light.

I jumped. I was at a pretty intense part of the book.

"*Here* you are, you goose," she said, sitting down on the

box of clothes beside my washtub. "I had a feeling you'd be up here! Find something good to read?"

I folded down the corner of the page I was on and nodded. "Hi, Gran."

"Hi, yourself!"

"I'm sorry I ran off. It's nice to see you."

Gran raised an eyebrow. *"Nice?"*

I shrugged.

Gran said, "Kiddo, let's be honest with each other, shall we?"

I shrugged again. I really didn't want to *talk* talk. Not even to Gran. I'd been fine up here reading my book. Alone.

Gran rumpled my hair and said, "While it's *nice* to see you too, Rebecca, and while you are always welcome here, these circumstances are hardly ideal, are they?"

I shook my head. I shook it again so that my hair would unrumple itself. My eyes felt itchy. From the dust, I told myself.

Gran sighed. "Yeah, this just plain old sucks, doesn't it?"

I nodded, but I still didn't open my mouth. My eyes wanted to water. I could tell.

Gran reached out and brushed something off my cheek. "Can't say I blame you, running off like that, but can you do me a favor?"

"I'm *not* talking to Mom. Not until she takes me home."

"Fair enough. Fair enough," said Gran. "I'm not trying

to get in the middle of what's between you and your mom. I only want you to promise you'll turn the lights on if you come up here to read. You're welcome to anything in this house. You can hang out anywhere you like, and ignore your mother for weeks on end like *I* do." Gran paused after she said that, waiting for me to laugh at her joke.

I made myself smile.

She finished by saying, "Heck, you can start a family feud if you like, but I *don't* want you ruining your eyesight under my roof. Understand?"

I couldn't help smiling for real then. It was a very Gran thing to say. "Okay," I said. "I promise."

"Good." She stood up and leaned over to kiss me on the head. "Now that we've got that important matter settled," she said, dusting off the seat of her jeans, "I wonder if you'd like to walk with us to the zoo after all? You don't have to, mind you, and I'll understand if you need more time alone. You're a big girl, and I trust you here by yourself if that's what you want. But there's a new baby panda, and we're going to stop for dinner after at my favorite Mexican place. So maybe you want to join us?" She winked at me and added, "I'll let you have a sip of my sangria when your mom isn't looking."

"Well . . . ," I said, groaning and standing up from the washtub. "Okay, but I'm not promising to talk to everyone."

"Of course not! Nobody expects you to talk to *everyone,*" said Gran. "To be honest, as far as I'm concerned, *everyone* is overrated."

When she said that, I laughed out loud for the first time in days. A for-real laugh, like, "Ha-ha-ha!" It felt like stretching.

CHAPTER 4

Gran clomped down the stairs. "She's coming with us, Annie!" she yelled ahead of her. "But you'd better behave yourself, and remember that I'm on *her* side!"

I was just about to follow Gran down the stairs with my book when I noticed the red bread box again, its letters shining silver. I could see them better now. The roses gleamed in the light. I couldn't stop looking at it.

"Gran!" I called down the stairs. "Hey, Gran! Can I bring this box downstairs with me? The red one?" I wasn't sure why I wanted the box, but suddenly I did. I had no clue what I'd do with it. Maybe I'd just store things in it, like books or snacks. I liked that it wasn't pink.

Gran stopped at the bottom of the stairs and looked back up, over her shoulder. She paused for a minute, like she was thinking about it. "The red one?" she asked. "Why that one?"

"I just like it," I said. "I think it's pretty."

"Oh," she said. "Well, sure, darlin'. I haven't set foot up here in months. I guess anything you want from this old attic is yours. I've a mind to burn the whole place down for insurance money."

I carried the red bread box down the stairs and set it on the desk in the pink room I was sleeping in, which I was sure would never feel like *my* room. Though someone, probably Mom, had laid a suitcase full of my clothes on the bed, so I was able to at least put on clean jeans and a fresh shirt.

I brushed my teeth and hair, which felt weird to do, since the day was half over. After that I walked for what felt like miles with Gran, Mom, and Lew. We hiked to the zoo, through a neighborhood of tall trees and very few people. We walked past big houses, most of them with enormous, wide porches and picket fences around their little front yards. Some of the houses were beautiful, with gingerbread-looking cutouts on the roofs, and some were falling-down dumps. Many had broken stained glass in them. The sidewalks were cracked and uneven, made of little concrete hexagons instead of big squares, with grass growing through the cracks. I played a kind of hopscotch on the way, trying to jump from hexagon to hexagon without tripping.

Later—after the pandas and the elephants, a long walk to a place called Holy Taco, two brisket tacos, some chips, a fizzy limeade, and churros with chocolate sauce, all of which I inhaled because I'd missed lunch while I was holed up reading—I found myself thinking about my afternoon in the attic. Why hadn't the red bread box been dirty and rusted over like everything else?

I sat in the restaurant, staring at Lew, who was covered in guacamole, and thought about that. It hit me that the red box had looked totally new, shiny. How could that be?

When we got back to the house, I headed straight for my room. The bread box was still there, glowing on the desk, as clean and shiny as I remembered. It was such a rich red color, with the silver letters so bright and the painted roses so lush, but besides being clean and pretty, there wasn't much else to it. It was a bread box. There wasn't much to say about a bread box.

I opened it up, and it was clean on the inside too, and empty. I decided that maybe it was just made of some special kind of metal or covered in some fancy dust-deflecting paint, so I headed back to the living room to watch TV with Gran, a special about the Civil War on PBS, which was the only channel she ever seemed to watch.

Eventually I got bored with listening to someone read dead people's letters over old-timey music, and went to my room. I burrowed under the covers with my Agatha Christie book, returning to the story of two young detectives in London. Much better! When Gran came in to say good night, I blew her a kiss and kept reading. I thought I'd already figured out who the villain was, but just to be sure, I read and read until the clock said it was 2:00 a.m. and I was done. Then I set the paperback down, flipped over on my side, and closed my eyes. I could feel myself starting to drift to sleep.

I had that nice *done* feeling of having finished a book, and I could still taste the chocolate from the churros on my lips because I'd forgotten to brush my teeth. It was very late at night. The window was open because it wasn't too cold out, just right for snuggling under a quilt. It almost felt like an actual vacation. Until I closed my eyes and began to drift off to sleep. Then memory hit me like a train—*whoomp*—and I saw Dad in the street, calling for us to come back.

I opened my eyes fast, but the feeling didn't go away. The sheets felt like his flannel shirt, soft against my skin. Sadness swallowed me like a bubble. It made my throat hurt. Dad was probably curled up in a ball right now, crying of loneliness, or at least asleep in his clothes on the couch. I could imagine it. He was lying there with the TV turned to nothing in particular, the remote falling out of his hand.

Suddenly the chocolate in my mouth tasted sour, not sweet. Like old food and spit.

I wondered if he'd gone to sleep clutching his phone. Two nights in a row I hadn't called him! I'd been busy laughing and reading and eating tacos. I was a terrible daughter.

It was too late to call now. I groaned. I rolled over again, burying my face in the pillow, and asked myself if this was how it would be forever: waves of feeling okay, or at least distracted, followed by waves of wanting to disappear into a hole. I promised myself I'd call him first thing in the morning, no matter what. I *would* call him.

I lifted my head and looked out the window, at the curtain blowing faintly in the dark room. It felt impossible and wrong. An open window in November might be nice, but it wasn't *home*. I missed home. Suddenly I was so tired, beyond tired, and I couldn't help it anymore. I wanted to be strong, I did, but the tears just came. Quietly. Rolling down my cheeks slowly. I was dripping. I dripped into my pillow so nobody would hear me. I dripped and dripped and held my locket in my hand, tugging it so that the chain bit into my neck. It hurt a little. It felt right that something should hurt a little.

I buried my face deeper into the pillow and mumbled into it, so that nobody would hear me, "I wish I were home. I wish I were home. I wish I were home." But of course wishing wouldn't make it so.

I dripped some more and said softly, "I wish this had never happened. I wish Dad were here." My soft pillow tasted like slobber and soap.

I choked through a face full of tears and snot. "I wish this was just vacation. I wish it was summer and we were at the beach, listening to the waves and watching the kites." My pillow was gross and I didn't care. I cried and dripped, and it felt good to say these things, to cry and miss. "I wish there were gulls."

And then—

I heard the noise!

From across the room, from inside the bread box on the desk, came a rumpled, ruffled, banging noise, followed by a *skrreeee!*

I jerked my head from my pillow and sat up. I pushed back the covers and jumped out of bed. I ran over to the desk and stared at the box.

It was moving slightly. The *skrreeee* came again. It was a weird noise, but I recognized it, so I reached out. I tugged on the door.

It burst open and out popped two dirty, angry seagulls, sort of tangled together. They pulled apart, unruffled themselves, glanced over at me, and then one of them screamed again. They were mad! They flew at my head, and I held up my arms and ducked.

Stiff feathers brushed my hair as both birds flew to the top of the bookshelf. They glared down at me with their little beady eyes.

Never taking my eyes off them, I inched over to the

window, my heart pounding out of my chest. With both hands, I slid open the screen. Then I stood very still. "I wished for gulls," I said softly.

Then I remembered something—that *The Secret Adversary* had appeared in the red box too, right *after* I'd wished out loud for a book to read.

Wow. Was it possible? It wasn't possible . . . was it?

I watched the gulls watching me from the bookshelf, and thought about things. After a minute, the birds flapped their wings and shot out into the soft Atlanta night, one after the other. I listened to them fly up into the dark sky with another *skrreeee.* I stared out the window after them. What would happen to them in this big unwatery city, stranded?

But the gulls had wings. They could fly home. I figured they'd work it out.

I turned back to the open bread box.

"I wish I had one hundred wishes!" I said, the words bursting out before I could decide if I actually believed in what was happening. Then my hand flew up to cover my mouth.

I'd spent years preparing for this moment. In fact, I'd kept a list in elementary school, when I was young enough to *really* believe in magic, a list of wishes I'd hoped to make someday, if I ever found magic. I'd wanted to make sure I got in lots of good wishes before my wishes ran out. Especially the more-wishes wish. I guess that little-girl list was still inside me somewhere, because when I saw the gulls, I wished right away.

Only I wasn't sure if it had worked or not. It was hard to know. Nothing happened. I didn't feel tingly or magical or anything. The bread box just sat there with its mouth open. How could I know if it had worked? Maybe the door to the box had to be closed for it to work. Both the seagulls and the book had appeared when the box was closed.

I shut the shiny red door, took a deep breath, and tried again. "I wish I had a magic wand," I said.

I opened the box. There *was* a magic wand inside, but it was just a piece of junk, a purple plastic toy. It was the kind of glittery wand little kids play with. I picked it up and waved it around my head. It made an annoying battery-powered thrumming sound. I tossed the wand to the floor and closed the box again. Lew could have *that*.

"I wish I had a *real* magic wand," I said. When I opened it this time, the box was empty.

I thought about that for a minute, closed the box door, and said carefully, "I wish I had a *real* unicorn horn."

I opened the box. No luck. Still empty.

I thought things over some more and closed the box again.

"I wish I had a cookie."

When I opened the box, I found an Oreo inside it.

Hmmm.

I ate the Oreo before I said, "I wish . . . I was home."

Nothing changed. Of course, *home* couldn't fit into a bread box. Besides, I'd wished for that already, hadn't I? Over and over, into my pillow. Before I'd wished for the gulls.

I tried to lick the inside of my mouth, which was now gummy and crumby and thick with frosting as I thought about what else I should wish for. Most of the wishes I'd had on my list as a kid weren't things I wanted anymore, not really. Or they were the kinds of things that apparently this box couldn't manage.

I yawned. I didn't want to be tired, but I was suddenly zonked, as Gran would say. Not to mention baffled by the magic and light-headed and drained like you get after you cry. It *was* three in the morning. In a few hours, Gran and Mom would be waking me up to go register at that stupid school.

But I couldn't fall asleep yet. Who goes to sleep when there's a box full of wishes?

I decided to try one more time. Just one more. One last wish. Then I'd go to bed.

"I wish I had," I began cautiously, "twenty dollars." Money is something people never wish for in books. Or if they do, they wish for too much and get buried or ruined by it.

When I opened the box this time, there *was* a bill inside it, as crisp as if it had just dropped from an ATM machine, and still slightly warm. I couldn't help grinning at the sight, because wands and unicorns aside, a girl can do a lot with an unlimited supply of money!

I snatched the bill out. Then I stood there with my hand on the box, and I couldn't help it. Just *one* more wish! Really. Just one more. I meant it this time. *Then* I'd go to bed.

"I wish I had . . . a thousand dollars," I said with my eyes shut and my fingers crossed. I opened my eyes, uncrossed my fingers, and opened the box very slowly.

Inside the box was dark, but whatever was in it was pushing against the door. I could feel the tension in my fingers, my wrist. I opened it a little farther and peered inside. I gasped. The box was stuffed with money! Not in neat stacks like you see in the movies, but crumpled and piled and squashed—a bread box full of loose bills! Old bills and new bills, singles and fives. All jammed together and spilling out of the box. Kind of the way wads of crumpled paper overflow a trash can after you finish an art project and then squash the mess down with your foot. It was the craziest thing I'd ever seen. So much money! What would I do with it all? My head swam from everything all at once.

I stuffed the twenty back into the box with the rest of the money, and then I took the whole bread box and tried to shove it into my suitcase. It didn't fit beside my clothes and shoes, so I dumped everything else onto the floor. Then I put the bread box in and pushed the suitcase under the bed. After that, I yawned again, the kind of yawn that makes your jaw ache. I climbed back into bed.

I needed to think this over. The possibilities were endless! I'd never be able to show anyone, because I'd never be able to explain it. But then, I didn't have to. Not here, not in Atlanta. This could be my secret. Because who did I have to tell? There wasn't anyone.

CHAPTER 5

I woke up to find Gran standing over me, swaying back and forth in a maroon jogging suit and singing, "Good morning to you! Good morning to you!" She was wearing earrings and lipstick, so I knew she was dressed up.

I looked at her and realized that I felt horrible—achy and tired and sick, like after a really late slumber party or three days with the flu.

Gran stopped singing. "Nice to see you've made yourself at home," she said, kicking at the pile of clothes on the floor.

When I saw all the things I'd dumped out of the suitcase—and the crappy plastic wand poking out of the pile—I remembered. I sat up right away, even though my bones hurt. "I'm up!" I shouted. "I'm up!"

"My, you certainly are," laughed Gran. "Looks like a good night's sleep did wonders for you. Something sure seems different about you today."

Something *was* different, though it wasn't a good night's sleep. It was the bread box—and the *thousand* dollars! Knowing that the day ahead was full of magic and money changed everything. I could almost *feel* the bread box in the room, waiting for me.

I was so distracted that I forgot to be mean to my mom at breakfast. When she asked me how I was feeling about registering for my new school, I didn't ignore her. I said I didn't know and ate my cereal, thinking about how, if I had to start at a new school, I'd at least be starting as a kid who could have anything she wanted. When Mom poured me a glass of grapefruit juice, I accidentally said thank you. Then I rushed to my room, but Gran knocked on the door and told me to get ready. I jumped into fresh clothes, but she was waiting for me, so that was all I managed to do before it was time to go. I barely had time to give Lew a squeeze on my way out the door. He was still in his pajamas, playing with some race cars in the hallway.

"Bye, Babecka," he said. Then he held up a car and grinned. "Vroom vroom vroomah!"

"Vroom," I said back.

Gran walked me to the school, an old-ish brick building a few blocks from the house. Because it was already late morning and school had started hours earlier, there were kids out on the blacktop, playing basketball behind a chain-link fence. They looked older than me.

Gran took me into the main office, where she introduced me to the lady sitting at the front desk. Gran called her Judy, but the nameplate on the lady's desk said her name was Mrs. Cahalen. She made a copy of the transcripts Mom had given Gran from my school in Baltimore, and I had to tell them my birthday and my old address, to make sure they had everything right. Mostly I just sat in a chair and stared into space, thinking about the transcripts and how Mom had been plotting all of this for a long time.

Then Mrs. Cahalen said, "We'll contact her old school next week, just to be sure everything is in order, but in the meantime she can go ahead to class. Okay?"

Gran said, "Okeydoke!"

"Huh?" I said. "No! Wait! I'm not starting today. It's Friday!"

And it wasn't only Friday. It was late morning, almost halfway through the school day. I'd just finished breakfast, but kids were probably on their way to lunch already. Anyway, nobody had said anything about me actually *starting* school today. Gran had only said we'd register. I'd been expecting a weekend of getting-ready time. Anyway, Dad and Mom could still work things out in time for me to go back to my real school on Monday. Mom had time to think things over. She hadn't started her new job yet. Anything could happen.

I looked up at Gran for help, but she just grinned and said, "Might as well get it over with! Right?"

Wrong.

"I don't even have a notebook with me. Or a pen," I protested.

"Oh, that's all right," said Mrs. Cahalen. "We can take care of you, Rebecca." She looked down at me with a smile and those I'll-be-your-friend-you-poor-thing-you sad eyes grown-ups make at kids. I knew Gran had probably told her all about my mom and dad. Gran was like Mom that way—she told everybody *everything.*

I could tell Mrs. Cahalen wanted to hug me or put her arm around me or something. I tried to frown at her just enough to be left alone but not enough to get in trouble with Gran.

"I'll be back for you in just a few hours," said Gran with a cheerful nod that was supposed to make everything okay. "Make some friends! Have fun!"

Fun?

What option did I have? There wasn't really anything I could do but march off after this Mrs. Cahalen person, down hallways full of art projects made by kids I didn't know. Past trophy cases and ugly banners. Into a classroom where a sea of strange eyes stared me down.

I took a deep breath and tugged at my shirt. I wished I'd worn my other jeans. They were nicer. Watching all those kids see me for the first time, it hit me that I was the New Girl. I'd never been the New Girl before. I'd always been a Since Kindergarten Kid.

Mrs. Cahalen handed me off with a too-long whisper to Mrs. Hamill, who introduced me as Becky to the class and then sat me down next to a girl with long blond hair. "This is Hannah," Mrs. Hamill said as she set down a beat-up science book, a pen, and a sheet of paper in front of me. "Hannah, you'll help Becky find her place, won't you?"

Hannah looked at me and nodded. I knew if there was ever going to be a moment to fix this Becky misunderstanding, it was now. I opened my mouth. Then I shut it again.

I didn't want to start out by correcting the teacher. I could be Becky for a few weeks. It wouldn't kill me. It might be nice to be someone besides me right now. A kind of disguise. Then, when we moved home, I'd go back to Rebecca, back to myself.

Hannah waved at me and said, "Hey, Becky," as Mrs. Hamill walked back to the front of the room. I could tell I'd gotten lucky. Not because Hannah was nice, though she seemed okay, but because Hannah was cool. Her hair was all shiny and layery. Her sneakers were just the right amount of broken in. She looked easy and fine, like she'd never been tossed into a car and driven halfway across the country at a minute's notice. She was just the kind of first friend the New Girl needed.

At home I'd always been a regular kid. I hadn't been

cool, but I hadn't gotten picked on either. Most of the time, Mary Kate and I kept to ourselves. We read a lot. We watched TV. We went to the park, and we liked to cook and bake together. Sometimes we hung out with a few other girls, for the purposes of birthday parties or school projects. I'd never cared about being part of the cool crowd of kids who walked together in a pack, hung around the deli drinking sodas before school, or spent their weekends at the mall.

Standing there, looking at Hannah's shimmery, lip-glossy smile, I had a feeling that I could be cool if I wanted. For however long I was here. I'd buy new clothes with my box of money. I'd be Becky Shapiro, the Cool New Girl from Up North. I was pretty sure I could pull it off, if I just didn't talk too much. That seemed important—not to talk too much. I'd be mysterious. Like Dad always said, "Less is more."

"Hi," I said, trying to look easy and fine too. I rolled my eyes at the ceiling for no reason and Hannah giggled. I shrugged my shoulders, and they felt like someone else's shoulders.

Off to a pretty good start.

The day was surprisingly okay after that. It was good to be busy and away from Mom. Mrs. Hamill mostly just talked. She reminded everyone that we needed permission slips for our visit to someplace called the Fernbank

Museum next month. Then she passed around handbooks for an experiment we were going to do on Monday: mixing a bunch of chemicals in plastic Baggies to see if they'd still weigh the same when they turned to gas. I tried not to laugh when she told us about it, because we'd just finished the same project at my school in Baltimore, and nobody had gotten the right results. You'd think teachers would try these things out at home first.

Still. I knew I would do as well as anyone, since I'd already passed one test on the law of conservation of mass. I figured as long as we *all* melted our Baggies, I didn't care how mine turned out. Mostly I spent the hour staring at the other kids as carefully as I could and trying to memorize the names Mrs. Hamill called out. There were two Madisons. Milo was the boy in the wheelchair.

Everyone seemed nice enough, but to me it was a weird class, different from home. Just like in Baltimore, there were all kinds of kids—black kids and white kids, Asian kids and kids with accents—but even though I knew this was a public school, these kids looked different somehow, more arty or something. Not like regular kids. A boy named Coleman had a Mohawk. Nobody at home in my grade had a Mohawk. I couldn't help thinking it was kind of cool. I don't know why, but I liked looking at the back of his head.

After class ended, it was time for lunch. I followed Hannah to what was clearly the cool-girls' table and set down my bag. Then I followed her through the line and ordered exactly what she ordered: a chicken salad sandwich and SunChips.

At the table, the other girls made a game out of teasing each other. Or that was what it seemed like to me anyway. They especially picked on a girl named Megan, who had supercurly bright red hair. They called it a 'fro and, giggling, tossed wadded-up straw wrappers at her head. When the bits of paper got stuck in her hair, everyone laughed, including Megan. But even though she was smiling, she didn't look like she was having too much fun to me.

Another girl, Maya, actually *did* have an Afro, but everyone seemed to think her Afro was cool. I guess it just wasn't cool on Megan. But I was the New Girl, so what could I do? I ate my chips carefully, trying not to drop crumbs, and smiled in a way that could or could not have been *at* Megan. I practiced being mysterious.

I tried not to look surprised when a girl named Cat talked about how she was "going out" with a boy named Henry. Henry was in eighth grade, she told me, and a good kisser—"not too slobbery." I tried not to blush when she said that. I don't think I succeeded, but I also think Cat kind of wanted me to be uncomfortable. Anyway, everyone was giggling a lot and glancing over at the table next to ours, which was, I guessed, where the cool boys sat. Coleman with the Mohawk was there.

After lunch we had gym class, where the other kids ran sprints and I didn't have to do anything but sit and observe, since I didn't have any gym clothes.

Then in English class, a really young-looking man named Mr. Cook read poems aloud and asked us over and over how the poems made us feel. I didn't want to be the one to answer him, since nobody else was saying anything, but I felt bad for him. He was trying so hard.

Actually, it was a little bit hard to look like I wasn't listening, because the poems were really good. A lot of them were about birds and made me think of the gulls, but I could tell they were about more than birds too. One of the poems was about horses, and I couldn't stop thinking of one summer when Dad and I went to Chincoteague and saw the wild horses.

"They love each other. There is no loneliness like theirs," read Mr. Cook.

I felt flutters inside. I could see the horses, lonely. I could see my dad on the beach. I couldn't stop thinking that line, like an echo.

Toward the end of the poem reading, Hannah passed me a note from three seats away. I was surprised to see the little folded-up square of paper appear on the corner of my desk. When I opened it up, it said, in extremely round letters, "How do I FEEL? Bored!"

When I looked over at Hannah, she was smirking at me, waiting for my response. I looked back down at the piece of paper and picked up my pen. I wasn't sure what to write back. I didn't feel bored myself, but of course the note passing was a good sign, so in my own roundest handwriting, I wrote back, "Ha!"

CHAPTER 6

"Hey, kiddo," said Gran when I met her in front of the school. "How was it?"

"Not too horrible," I said, walking quickly past a long line of parked minivans, toward the house and my bread box, and wishing Gran wasn't such a moseying person. I could tell she wanted to hear every little detail—what I ate for lunch and who I talked to and what my teachers were like. But I didn't want to say, "I sat with the cool kids at lunch and one of the girls was talking about kissing a boy and mostly I just kept my mouth shut so people would like me." I didn't think Gran would necessarily think those were good things, so I just said, "We read some poems."

"That's always nice," said Gran.

After that we moseyed some more. Gran pointed out a gravel alley where she said there was an urban farm with hives of bees and chickens too. "And the best dang rope

54

swing you ever saw!" she said. "We'll come back here with Lew sometime next week."

"He'd like that," I said, though I really hoped we'd be gone by next week.

Then Gran said, "Hey! What say we give your old dad a call when we get back to the house? Your mom is out with Lew. I think she took him to a movie."

"Oh no!" I stopped walking and stared at Gran.

"What? What's wrong?"

"Dad," I said. "I never called him. I meant to call this morning."

Gran patted my shoulder. "It's okay, kiddo. You've got a lot going on. He'll understand."

But would he? I'd forgotten again! How had I forgotten? I'd sworn to myself I'd call in the morning, but then I'd been so tired and distracted. All the goodness of the day—the coolness and the poems and even the bread box waiting for me—melted away. I ran the rest of the way to the house, with Gran panting to keep up. I bolted up the brick steps to the porch.

I still had to wait for Gran to let us inside and find her phone, which turned out to be in a bowl of apples on the kitchen counter, of all places. It was black, with paper scraps taped to the back of it, each of them scrawled with phone numbers.

"You know," I said to Gran as I dialed, "you can program the numbers *into* the phone."

Gran laughed. "Maybe *you* can. I can barely get used to having this thing at all. I got rid of my old-fashioned, regular, normal, perfectly fine phone when I bought this little gadget, and I find I can barely work the thing. In fact—"

The phone was ringing, so I ran to my room and shut the door behind me.

My hand shook a little as I waited for Dad to answer. It had been two days too many. I was scared he'd be mad at me.

At last he picked up. "Hello?" he asked. His voice was like usual, calm, happy-sounding. His voice was Home. I stopped shaking, but I couldn't seem to make any words come out.

"Hello?" he repeated. "Who's this?"

I wasn't sure why my mouth wasn't working.

"Hello?" he asked a third time. He sounded mildly irritated but surprisingly like his normal self, not at all like a man curled up in a lonely ball on the couch. "Helloooo? Anyone there?"

He was going to hang up if I didn't say something. So I managed to bleat out, "Dad?"

"Becks!" he yelled. "Monkey! How are you?"

It made me feel warm all over when he called me monkey. "Fine," I said. "I *guess* I'm fine, sort of. I miss you."

"Me too. Oh, man. So much I miss you. I didn't have your gran's number. I tried to look it up, but it's unlisted or something. And your mom's cell phone is going straight to voice mail. I've been going nutso not being able to get you guys on the phone. Tell her to charge that thing!"

"I will," I said. "I'm sorry."

"It's okay," he said. "It's not your fault. I'm just so glad to hear your voice!"

"I'm glad to hear yours," I said.

Then, without any warning, he got serious. "Don't worry, Becks. Your mom and me—we'll get it worked out. I want you guys home."

"I want to come home too," I said.

"I know you do," he said. "I know." His voice trailed off. Then he said, "But how was the drive? And how's every-thing going? Everything else, I mean . . ."

"Everything's awful." As I spoke that sentence, I knew it wasn't entirely true. That wasn't fair. Everything wasn't awful. Gran was great, of course, and school hadn't been so bad. Then there was the bread box. But my anger felt like something I could give him. I could say it was awful for him. Maybe it would even get me home sooner if I did. If I had a lot of fun, it would just be easier for Mom to feel okay about staying.

"I know, monkey, I know," he said softly. "I get it."

I touched Grandma Shapiro's locket with the hand that wasn't holding the phone.

He asked how Lew was doing, and I said he was fine, though the question made me realize I didn't really know because I hadn't been paying much attention to Lew. I'd been too busy thinking about other things. "Gran's been playing with him a lot," I added.

"And how's your mom doing?" he asked in a serious voice.

"I . . . don't know," I answered. I wasn't sure what he wanted me to say.

"No, no, I guess it isn't your job to know," he said softly.

"Anyway," I added, "I'm not really talking to her."

"Oh, Becks," he said. "This isn't how it's supposed to be. I'm so sorry."

"Well, it isn't *your* fault," I said.

He just laughed a weird little laugh then, like a breath with a laugh inside it. Then he changed the subject and told me about what was happening at home. He said that he'd started looking really hard for work and had a lead on a teaching job at a boys' high school.

That surprised me. Long ago, before he started driving his cab, Dad had been a history teacher at a college, but he always said he liked driving the cab better. He said the people in his cab were smarter than the people at the college. It made other grown-ups laugh when he said that.

"You're going to teach again?" I asked.

"Maybe. We'll see."

Dad said Mary Kate wanted him to tell me that she missed me. Now that he had Gran's number, he promised to give it to her. I told him I'd email her.

Dad said he'd cleaned the house, and he asked me to tell Mom, so I said I would. Then it was like he ran out of things to say. Since I didn't know what to say either, I told him I'd call again, when I could put Lew on the phone. I knew Lew wouldn't have much to say. He always gets quiet when you put the phone near his face. But it would make Dad happy, and Lew would smile when he heard Dad's voice.

When I said goodbye, Dad said, "There are things, Becks—your mom—I wish I'd done differently. . . ."

I wasn't sure how to respond to that, so I told him I was sending him a hug. Then I hung up the phone and sat on my bed, thinking. I was glad I'd called. I was relieved that he was okay and that he was doing all the things Mom wanted. I felt better. Ten times better. A hundred times better. One little phone call and I felt like me again.

So I pushed a chair under the doorknob like people do on TV. I wrestled the bread box out of the suitcase and set it on my bed. I took out all the money, smoothed and folded the bills, then bound them in bundles using ponytail holders. It felt good to get everything organized. I buried the bundles under my clothes in the suitcase. After that I sat down on the bed, cross-legged, and stared at the empty bread box.

I wished for a bunch of things right away, things I'd been wanting forever. I wished for an iPod and got it. I wished for a supersize bag of Twizzlers and ate them while I wished for a phone of my own so I wouldn't have to ask Gran for hers anymore. When the phone arrived, it was purple.

The wishing was nuts. Practically anything I wanted I could have! It was like my birthday, with no bad gifts.

Then it occurred to me that I'd have to explain where I was getting all these things, so I stopped and tried to think of tiny things I wanted. I knew if I wished for something hard to hide—like a computer or a kitten—I was sure to get busted. I tried to think of small things worth having. I couldn't think of many. What was tiny and wonderful?

At last I said, "I wish for . . . a diamond."

A *diamond*?

I reached across the bed and opened the box. Inside it was a diamond, a real diamond! I—Rebecca Rose Shapiro—owned a diamond of my own! How crazy was that?

I sat holding my diamond cupped in my hand for a bit. I wasn't sure what to do with it. What do you *do* with a diamond? Especially a diamond you can't tell anyone about?

I climbed off the bed and carefully placed the diamond in a tiny box on the dresser, a little pink butterfly-shaped box that had probably been my mom's when she was a kid. I hid the Twizzlers bag in the suitcase with the money and the phone. I set the iPod—which had come loaded with songs I'd mostly never heard of before—to shuffle. Then

I lay back on my pink pillow and listened to the music, glancing now and then at the unfamiliar names of the bands.

I really liked a group called The Flaming Lips, even though I thought they had a weird name. Their songs were kind of bouncy and floaty, and I was so tired from my late night that I fell asleep listening to them. I was still lying there, snoozing on my pink bed with the plastic red taste of Twizzlers on my tongue, when a song woke me up. *The* song. *Dad's* song. The song that was emblazoned in my brain more deeply than any other song ever could be. I heard it and opened my eyes.

It was the song that the three of us—on good nights when my parents were still getting along, before Lew was even born—had danced to in the living room before bed. Mom would dim the lights and Dad would push PLAY on the CD player on the fireplace mantel and we'd all dance. I'd stand on the coffee table and my parents would hold my hands. I'd belt out the words. I knew them by heart, which was funny, because I'd never really *thought* about the words before, though I'd sung the song all my life.

Suddenly wide-awake, I stared at the ceiling as I sang along under my breath. I couldn't stop myself. What a weird coincidence! *That* song, sent to me now, as if by magic. I felt like there was a ghost in the room. How had the bread box known?

Got a wife and kids in Baltimore, Jack.
I went out for a ride and I never went back . . .

I'd always loved to shout out the word *Baltimore* with
my dad. As if the fact that it was about *our* city made it
somehow *our* song, as if the fact that anyone would write
a song about our dirty city made it less dirty. Made us
famous. Made us matter.

I sang along with those words, and it was like I'd never
heard them before in my life. How had I never paid attention until now? *Kids? Never went back?* I'd never thought
about the kids before, or the never going back. It had only
been a song to jump around to with the lights down. It
was a loud song, a dancing kind of song. The kind of song
you played air guitar to. Dad always pretended he had a
saxophone.

I stopped singing along and listened carefully.

Like a river that don't know where it's flowin',
I took a wrong turn and I just kept goin' . . .

Who would *do* that? Keep going after a wrong turn?
What kind of person stayed away? And why? The voice in
the song sounded so sad, so hungry, even though the
music was fast. Why didn't he just go back? I thought
about my mom. I couldn't help it.

Everybody's got a hungry heart.
Everybody's got a hungry heart.
Lay down your money and you play your part.
Everybody's got a hu-u-ungry heart.

I pulled out my earbuds and buried the iPod beneath the pillow, but I couldn't get rid of the feeling that something was wrong.

I tried to remind myself of Dad on the phone, saying that he was looking for a job, that he might even go back to teaching, which would make Mom *so* happy. I thought about Dad saying he missed me. I thought about my mom saying she just needed to think things over. I reminded myself that I had a bread box full of wishes. It would all be *fine*. Everything would work out. I told myself that.

But underneath all that was the song, repeating. I couldn't block the memory of the three of us, dancing in the warm light of the living room. My parents laughing. My mother's head tossed back so that her hair hung down her back. My father's big warm hand holding my hand, holding me up, balanced, so that I didn't fall off the coffee table. I remembered knowing that I would never fall off. I knew, I knew, I *knew* that they loved each other. Didn't we all want to be happy still? Together? How could they ever work things out if they weren't together? Why were we so far apart?

Right then my mom startled me, yelling out, "Rebecca, please come help us set the table for dinner!" And I remembered why.

Even so, I headed for the door, because suddenly I needed to get away from the song, and my thoughts. However I felt about Mom, I wanted to be in the warm kitchen with everyone. I didn't want to be alone, but I wasn't going to talk to her, like I had at breakfast. I wasn't going to talk to her until she fixed things and took us home.

Still, it was nice to eat the chicken noodle casserole that she and Gran had made. It was good to hear them talking about nothing much. It felt normal. I sat next to Lew and watched him make a mess of his plate. I couldn't help laughing at him, all covered in chicken glop. Whatever else was different, Lew was the same. He was two and I was twelve, but we were both stuck in this place together. We played I Spy as we ate, and then I wiped his face and hands. After dinner, Gran and I read picture books to Lew on the couch, while Mom did the dishes.

I didn't touch the bread box again that night.

CHAPTER 7

The next morning, Gran woke me up again, but this time she didn't sing. She didn't say anything. In fact, I'm not even sure quite why I woke up. I guess I could just feel the weight of her, sitting on my bed, silently waiting for me to wake up. It was weird.

I opened one eye. "You aren't going to sing at me again today?" I asked her.

"Saturday," she said. "Doesn't seem right on Saturday. Everyone else is still in bed, so I thought I'd let you rest a little longer. I was just looking at you, thinking how much you remind me of your mother when she was your age."

I shifted and rolled over so that she wasn't sitting on my foot. She moved and sat on my other one.

"Actually," I said, closing my eyes again, "I look a lot more like Dad. Also, this isn't really sleeping. You woke me up, and now you're sitting on my foot."

"Oh," she added, shifting her weight back to the first foot. "Well, generosity was my *plan,* but then I came in to watch you sleep—because that's the weird sort of thing grandmothers do—and I realized I wanted to talk to you about something. So here we are."

"Okay," I said, propping myself up on my elbows. "What did you want to talk about?"

"Well," Gran said, "with all the commotion, it makes sense that you'd forget. I mean, you're a kid, and there's been a lot going on. Nobody's mad at you or anything. . . . I don't want to make you feel bad at all . . . and I didn't say anything at first. . . ."

"Mad at me for what?" I asked.

"Your mom's birthday," said Gran.

I sat up the rest of the way. "It's *today?*" The last thing I wanted to do was *celebrate* my mom.

Gran shook her head.

"Well, then, when is it?" I asked, falling back into my pillows.

"It was *last* week."

"Last week?" I sat up again. "But nobody reminded me. Nobody said anything."

"Well," she sighed, "it is *possible* you would have just remembered on your own. It isn't like you're five years old anymore." I started to protest, to argue, but she held up a hand and continued. "But you're right. Nobody said anything, or did anything, and I think that was the straw that broke the camel's back. Her birthday was Tuesday."

"Tuesday." I thought back, counting the days. Tuesday had been the day before Suitcase Day.

"Don't feel bad, kiddo. It really isn't your fault. You could have remembered, and that would have been nice, but *you* aren't really the issue. Your dad blew it big-time."

"But is *that* why we're here? Because he forgot her birthday? That's an awful reason, and anyway, it seems like she'd been planning—"

Gran smiled a weak smile. "Honey, I doubt he just forgot. I'm betting he was sending her a message loud and clear, but even if he just forgot, it made her feel bad. Anyway, no reason is ever *the* reason for something like this. It was the excuse your mom needed to make her move. She hasn't been . . . very happy. I guess you could say she'd been weighing her options."

"Why?" I asked, thinking about the fight they'd had when the lights went off, remembering the things Mom had said in the dark. Without meaning to, I reached for my locket and clutched it in one hand.

Gran's eyes followed my fingers. "You have to ask her about that, but I think her well kind of ran dry. Nobody else was helping to fill it. So she got tired of drawing water for everyone else. You get me?"

"Not really," I said. Wasn't it a mom's job to get the water?

Gran sighed. "It's funny, Rebecca, how badly moms need presents. They do a lot they never get thanked for, so little things become big. Presents matter. In good ways and in bad ways. I betcha a lot of marriages have come undone after birthdays or anniversaries. Come to think of it, I almost left your grandfather one Christmas."

"Because he didn't get you a present?"

"Well, more because he didn't get your *mom* a present, and because he had been a grouch all dang day, and because he never put the tree up even though he said he would. But that's another story, and anyway, he left a few months later. It was for the best, really. It wasn't like I couldn't support myself, and besides, he wasn't very much fun."

I tried to digest all that. I didn't know much about my grandfather. In fact, this was as much as anyone had ever told me about him directly. I only knew that he'd gone away when Mom was a kid and that he'd been a lawyer, and bald, and that his name had been John, and that we didn't really talk about him.

Now I wondered if there would ever be a good time to ask Gran more about him. But before I could think more about it, Gran changed the subject back to Mom's birthday. She handed me a ten-dollar bill and said, "You don't have to get her anything fancy, but here, I thought maybe today or tomorrow we could run around town, and you could pick her out a little present. Surprise her with it at a special dinner. Make her feel good."

I scowled. I wasn't feeling so mad at my mom anymore, not like I had been a few days ago, but I wasn't ready to do nice things for her either. If I gave her a present, she'd think things were all fine again. She'd expect me to start talking to her again for real. I wasn't ready for that.

"Look, kiddo," said Gran. "Your mom has made a mess of things, but she loves you more than anything in the world, and she's having a hard time too right now. This isn't easy on her."

"Then she shouldn't have done it!" I said.

"That might be true," said Gran. "But sometimes it doesn't matter whether someone is right or wrong. Sometimes you just have to love them when they need you."

"I'm not sure I can right now."

"Maybe you can try seeing this as a chance for you to grow up a little, Rebecca. By which I mean . . . maybe you can try to fake it."

I scowled again.

"You can be mad at her all you want. You have that right. But happy or sad, you're going to have to do some stretching. She'll need help with Lew, and even if your parents work things out, nothing will be the same when you get home. You're not a little girl anymore. This changes things. You and your mom are going to be partners now, in a way. Are you ready for that?"

"I'm not sure," I said.

"Well, then, *get* sure," said Gran. "Now show your

mom you understand, and get her some silly thing so we can have a birthday dinner for her tomorrow night. It doesn't matter what it is. A coffee mug. Some bath salts. A candle. Whatever it is people get their moms these days. I certainly don't know what that is. But it'll be a very big deal to her, I'll betcha. And that will make all our lives easier."

"Fine. I'll get her *something*," I sulked.

"Good girl," said Gran. "Smart girl."

"But I'm still not talking to her," I added.

"Suit yourself. That'll only make things harder for you," said Gran.

I didn't think so. "Anyway, you know what?" I said, looking up at my grandmother. "I talked to Dad, and he cleaned the house. Also he's looking for a job. A good one."

Gran sighed. "I hope for everyone's sake that's true. I like your dad. I always *have* liked him. He's basically a good guy. But sometimes, Rebecca, a person goes so far down a road, they can't find the energy to walk back the other way." Then Gran stood up and walked out of the room.

I took the ten dollars, even though I didn't need it. Then I decided to spend the entire day watching TV alone. In my room. On the mini TV I wished for next. It was a risky wish, but I thought I deserved it. When it arrived in my room, it was kind of old and dusty, so I figured I could always say I'd found it in the attic. That was very nearly true.

Chapter 8

The next day was Sunday, and everyone slept in—except Lew, who came into my room, dragging his blanket, and crawled into bed with me. After Mom and Gran woke up, we all walked to a coffee shop called Joe's for a late breakfast. Joe's was full of broken-down velvet couches, weird cartoony art, and scratched coffee tables. It was colder outside than it had been all week, and windier, almost like home. A reminder that winter was coming, even though the trees still looked like fall. I wore my coat.

A guy with messy, complicated hair was working behind the counter. He had a cool dragon tattoo on his neck, and he looked mean, but he seemed friendly when he asked what we wanted. I ordered a chocolate muffin, which is just a cupcake without icing. When I sat down to eat it, my new phone and the big wad of money in my back pockets made it uncomfortable to sit, even on the squishy sofa. I wasn't sure why I'd brought the phone along, since I couldn't exactly use it in front of Mom and Gran, but you never know when you'll need to make a call.

Lew had fresh-squeezed tangerine juice and part of my mom's scone, and he made a huge mess all over the carpet, but nobody seemed to care. While I helped him clean up the crumbs, Mom read the paper and Gran just settled back into the couch. It all felt very Sunday.

After a while, Gran winked at me and said to my mom, "I think maybe Rebecca would like to go off by herself for a bit. Poor kid's been stuck with us old folks and babies all morning!"

"I not a baby," said Lew, pouting.

Mom set down the paper. "I'm not so sure. She doesn't know the area at all."

"I'm twelve, Mom," I said. "What do you think will happen to me if I leave for a measly hour? Anyway, Baltimore is way rougher than Atlanta!" I wasn't so sure if that was actually true. The guy in the biker jacket, muttering to himself by the door, kind of gave me the creeps.

"Give her an hour, Annie," said Gran firmly, laying a hand on my mom's arm. "The village runs only two blocks in either direction. Not much trouble to get into, and she'll be careful. Right, Rebecca? Look both ways?"

I nodded.

With a big, exasperated sigh, my mom said yes and

went back to her paper. So I walked out of the coffee shop. The door creaked behind me when I shut it.

On the street, I felt invisible but also tingly at the thought of being completely on my own in a place like this. Most of the buildings housed funky-looking bars that weren't open yet, and most of the people who walked past me looked like they were in rock bands. Everyone seemed to be either moving too quickly or too slowly. A lot of people were walking dogs. The dogs all looked strangely related, shovel-headed, with thick, strong bodies, either black or brown.

I stopped to pet one of the dogs. The pretty lady holding his leash smiled at me. "His name is Petey. He likes you," she said as the dog licked at my face. His warm breath and his whiskers tickled me, and I decided that if I ever got home, I might ask my dad for a dog.

After that, I walked slowly down the line of shops, staring in the windows. In the only bar open at eleven o'clock in the morning, a woman with purple hair was playing a banjo while the guy beside her, in overalls and an old-fashioned mustache, played an electric guitar. The people watching them were eating omelets and drinking cans of beer. I thought that was weird, but I liked the music. The lady had a soft, pretty voice that reminded me of campfires.

I walked past the window of a gift shop and was drawn in by some blue pottery. I wandered around in the shop for about five minutes, but even with the amount of money in my pocket, it was too expensive for Mom's gift. If I spent fifty dollars on a vase, Gran would wonder what was going on. Before leaving the store, I took a deep whiff of the warm candles-and-wood smell. It was a nice place, and I wished I had someone with me to show it to. They had a wall of goofy, dirty greeting cards by the door. I knew if Mary Kate were here, we'd read them to each other and laugh at the bad words and funny photos. I made a mental note to email Mary Kate later. For some reason, I was nervous to call her. I didn't know what I'd say. There was too much to say.

I passed another bar and a sushi restaurant. They were both closed. Then I came to a tiny store that smelled spicy, like the Indian dress shop in Baltimore where Mary Kate's big sister Colleen bought her clothes. It made me homesick, that smell, but happy too. I went in.

The store was crammed full of knickknacks and old clothes, junky jewelry, and bad, dusty art. I pawed around for a bit before a woman in a lacy vintage party dress came out from the back and asked if she could help me.

"I need a present," I said, "for my mom."

"Well, what does she like?" asked the woman, fiddling with a dangly silver earring.

My mom worked at the hospital and she made dinner and she went to the grocery store and she read to Lew, and that was about all I could think of. When she was really tired at the end of the day, she watched reruns of *Law and Order* on TV and had a glass of wine.

"She likes wine," I said.

I knew that wasn't really true. She didn't like wine any more than she liked coffee, really. Coffee and wine were just the way she started and ended most of her days. But I didn't know what else to say.

"Oh, I have just the thing," said the woman, digging around on a shelf until she found a dusty glass vase kind of thing. She held it in a funny, careful way, lightly, because her fingernails were really long and pointy. They were also dark purple.

"What's that?" I asked.

"It's a decanter," said the woman.

"What's it for?" I asked.

"You pour your wine into it," she said.

"Then what?" I asked.

"Then you pour it into your glass and drink it," said the woman.

I stared at her. "You pour your wine from one bottle into another bottle, just so you can pour it into your glass?"

The woman nodded. She looked amused with me. I didn't like amusing her, so I didn't say anything else. I just turned and left. I didn't think my mom liked wine like *that*.

After that, I passed a used bookstore with an orange cat in the window, but I was pretty sure my hour was about up; besides, I didn't have any clue what books Mom hadn't already read or what she'd want. She read a lot, mostly books with women on the covers, but I couldn't exactly walk in and say "I need a book with a woman on the cover" any more than I could say "I need a book for a mom." I stared through the window at a guy behind the counter, fiddling with his glasses. He couldn't really have any idea what Mom wanted, unless he was psychic or something.

I didn't think that was very likely, but wishing he was psychic gave me a brilliant idea. I left the window of the bookstore right away and hurried back to Joe's, where I plopped down next to Lew and drank the last slurp of his juice.

"Vroom zoom zoom!" said Lew, holding up a red race car.

"Zoom!" I said back.

He giggled.

"Mission accomplished?" asked Gran in a whisper as we walked home.

"I think so," I said, nodding and walking faster.

At the house, I went to my room and shoved the chair back under the door. I was getting good at that trick. Then I turned to the bread box.

"I wish . . . ," I said. "I wish I had the perfect present for my mom."

I wasn't sure if this would work. It felt like cheating to have the box do the work of thinking up a gift, but when

I opened the door, there *was* something inside: a tiny little spoon, tarnished and bent. A spoon?

Of course! A spoon!

I never would have thought to get her one, but the minute I saw the spoon, I knew she'd love it. I almost didn't want to give it to her, knowing how happy she'd be when she saw it. Mom had collected spoons forever. She had a wooden miniature shelf thing on the wall in the living room at home, where her spoons hung. She'd been collecting them since she was a kid.

I reached into the box and wondered what made this spoon so special, so perfect. Why *this* spoon? I took it out and held it up to the light for inspection. It was cold, like it had been sitting outside somewhere. The bowl of the spoon was thin and fine, like paper almost. The silver had a yellowish sheen to it. It was a nice-enough old spoon, but it wasn't nearly as fancy as some of the spoons she already had. Some of them were engraved with windmills or had vines creeping up them. When I was little, I'd played with Mom's spoons. My favorite had been one that looked like a boat.

I turned the spoon over. On the back was a little scrawl of cursive. It said, *To Adda. From Harlan. With love.* Who were Harlan and Adda? The spoon looked pretty old to me.

I was a genius. The *bread box* was a genius! My mom would love this. She'd love that it was old, and she'd love the inscription. Most of all she'd love it because I'd thought of it. Which of course I hadn't, but whatever . . .

I went to find a piece of paper to wrap it in. I didn't have a card, but there was nothing I wanted to say to her that you could put on a birthday card.

That night, Gran served steak and cake. "Steak and cake!" she shouted as she brought the cake, covered with candles, into the room. "That's what makes a party. Am I wrong?"

I didn't know about that, but the steak was perfect, hot off the grill in the backyard. The meat sizzled, juicy and tender. Beside a mound of homemade mashed potatoes. We never had steak at home. Dad said we couldn't afford steaks worth eating.

I have to admit: It's hard not to be happy when you're eating a big steak.

And the cake! The cake was incredible. Towering and rich and dark and covered in tall, skinny candles. My mom looked happily at me through the candles as we sang, and I managed not to scowl back at her. The candles were shining and her eyes were shining and she clapped her hands like Lew does when he's really excited.

I couldn't help thinking that Mom was usually the person who lit the candles, and baked the cake too. I wasn't even sure what we'd done for her last birthday, now that I thought about it. I watched her, and then I looked over at Gran and saw that Gran was just as happy as Mom.

We tore into that cake. It tasted as amazing as it looked. Three layers of moist cake with chunks of bitter-sweet chocolate and fudge icing. A ribbon of raspberry ran through the cake, and Lew managed to smear it all over his nose somehow. We all laughed.

"This is the best cake ever," I said to Gran.

"That's because nobody you know made it," said Gran. "I leave important things like cake baking to the experts."

Then it was time for presents.

Gran gave Mom a new red leather wallet to replace her ratty old one, which had ink marks all over it from being in her gigantic purse with a lot of leaky pens.

Lew gave Mom a card he'd made (which meant that Gran had made it and forced Lew to draw on it, but still . . .). Mom oohed and aahed and tickled him and gave him a kiss. He giggled a lot and said, "Welpum! Welpum!"

After Lew was done being cute, I gave Mom my tiny present, folded in newspaper. She held it lightly in one hand, like she was weighing it with her fingers. "I wonder what this could be?" she said with a smile.

I stared at my cake plate and used my fork to draw a flower in the frosting smeared there.

"So do I!" said Gran, sounding more excited than Mom. "Open the darn thing!"

Mom pulled the piece of tape off one end and peeked in. Then she stared up at me, without opening it the rest of the way. "Rebecca! Oh. Gosh. Really?"

"What *is* it?" asked Gran.

"Yah, wha is?" said Lew, peeking curiously over her arm.

Mom slid the spoon out into her palm and held it up for the others to see. "It's a Gorham!" she said. "It's a really rare spoon. A really special spoon. And look, there's writing." She read it aloud: "'To Adda. From Harlan. With *love.*'" She looked at me and then back down at the spoon. "Wow," she said. She looked stunned.

I was almost happy that she was so happy. She seemed so grateful. I was also a little surprised at just *how* happy she was. It didn't take much with moms, I guess. She was *really* happy.

"It's just a spoon," I said with a shrug. "I remembered you like little spoons."

"It's not just a spoon," said my mom. "It's *the* spoon. The perfect spoon. The spoon I've always wanted. How did you know?" She turned to Gran. "Did you remember? Did you help her pick this out?"

Gran shook her head. "Nope. Not a bit. What do I know about spoons?"

Mom turned back to me and shook the spoon in the air, seeming almost a little angry. "How did you afford this?" she asked me. "This spoon is worth more than— Well, it's worth a lot!"

I didn't know what to say. I hadn't thought that part through. I shifted in my chair.

"Rebecca?" My mom was now staring at me in a

not-entirely-happy way and holding out the spoon. "Just how did you buy this?"

Then I remembered the junky little store in the village and that silly wine bottle lady. "A junk store!" I said quickly, with relief. "I bought it at a junk store. I didn't know. I mean, I just thought it was an old spoon, like your other spoons. It hardly cost anything at all. Gran gave me the money."

"Wow," said my mom. "Really?" She smiled again, and the wrinkles disappeared from her forehead. "That's a lucky find. I mean, *really* lucky. These are rare!"

I squirmed. I wasn't a very good liar, but I certainly wasn't going to tell them about the bread box.

"Well, then, good job, kiddo!" said Gran, standing up to clear the table. "You outdid me for sure!" She winked.

"Yay, Babecka!" said Lew.

My mom looked at me thoughtfully as she ran her thumb around the worn bowl of the spoon. "You know, I've been hunting thrift stores and yard sales all my life for one of these. For this very spoon. My grandma Molly collected spoons before me, and I inherited her collection. That's how I got started. But this was the one she was hunting, and here it is, waiting for me, here all the while. Back in Atlanta, just a few blocks from home. It's almost like . . . almost like a good omen. Almost like we were supposed to come home—to find it. Almost like we're supposed to be here."

"Um, yeah, I guess . . . ," I said. That didn't sound

good to me at all, but I had to admit that it was interesting to hear Mom talk about her grandmother, the same way it had been interesting to hear Gran talk about my grandfather the day before. Something about being in Gran's house was bringing these long-gone people to life. Molly? Was she the same Molly from the picture in the attic? Molly with the red dress and the sad eyes? I'd never heard a word about her before. I wished, not for the first time, that my parents talked more about their families. I liked old pictures. I liked stories. I liked other people's relatives, and if I ever had a chance to meet them, I was pretty sure I'd like my relatives too. I only had Gran. Oh well.

Later, I was lying in bed in the dark when the door opened. Mom hadn't tried to tuck me in since we'd gotten to Gran's house. I hadn't wanted her to, but I was almost glad to see her dark shape in the doorway, outlined with light. It looked . . . familiar. I wasn't ready to talk to her about anything that was going on with me, but if she wanted to thank me for the present again, I guess I'd let her.

"Rebecca?" she whispered. "You still awake?"

"Yeah," I said. I turned to look at her as she walked over. "I'm sorry I forgot your birthday."

She sat down on the edge of my bed. "Oh, that's fine. But thank you, Rebecca, for saying that. I'm glad you're . . . adjusting. I've . . . missed you."

I turned away from her. "Know what?" I said. "Dad's

looking for a job. He told me so. He might go back to teaching. And he cleaned the house."

"That's nice, dear," she said to my back, but she didn't sound like she meant it. Or maybe she didn't sound like she believed me. "I need to call your father. We should talk. I'll call him tomorrow. Okay?"

"Okay," I said, still facing away.

That should have made me happy, but it didn't. Mom didn't sound very excited to call Dad, so I added, "It'll be nice, once we're home. Won't it? Once things are better? And we can go back to normal?"

She took a minute before she said, "I hope so. Maybe. We'll see."

I didn't say anything else. I closed my eyes hard, and she kissed the back of my head. There was nothing more I wanted to say. I turned over and breathed into my pillow, until it felt all warm and smothery.

I didn't move, so finally she left, closing the door carefully behind her with a click.

CHAPTER 9

After that, things started to feel almost normal, as long as I didn't think too much about the fact that I was in a strange place and my dad wasn't there and I was pretty much all alone. At home I wasn't exactly *talking* to my mom, but I wasn't *not* talking to her anymore either. She started working at a hospital downtown, but she said it was a really rough place to work and it wore her out. Since she was just filling in for other people, she mostly got lousy shifts. She was working late at night and sleeping a lot during the day, and I could see she wasn't happy. It made me feel a little better about everything. That's mean, I know, but sometimes the truth just is. The sooner she got sick of Atlanta, the sooner we'd go home.

I walked to school in the mornings. During lunch and in the hallways, I hung out with Hannah and her friends and tried not to mess up being Becky. I almost never raised my hand in class, but my teachers were good, and the classes were interesting. Really, it was fun, like I was playing a game. I felt like I was keeping a secret all the time. I tried to think of it as a magical vacation. Sooner or later, I'd go home.

I paid attention to what the other kids wore, and thanks to the bread box, I got some new clothes for myself. That was always fun, the wishing! Things I didn't think Mom would notice. Better jeans. New tennis shoes. An expensive hoodie like some of the other girls had, but in gray like my old ratty one so it would blend in. Nothing too fancy. Nothing that called attention to itself. I also managed a few small things I wanted, like a cool silver watch. Little things. Each time I wished and then something appeared in the box, I got a shiver down my spine. It never got old.

It took me a while to think of it, but eventually I realized that the best way to use the bread box was to wish for things I could give away. Of course, Mom and Gran couldn't notice the things I didn't keep. So I wished for fancy chocolates, which I took to school and handed out in the cafeteria. I wished for handmade beaded hair ties that Hannah said she liked. Soon everyone had a pair. My pockets were always full of gum. I always had an extra pen handy. When someone borrowed my lip gloss in the bathroom, I was able to say, "Oh, here. You can have it. I have a bunch of them!" It was nice, sharing. It was nice when people said thank you. I always had lunch money to spare when people needed to borrow. I was rich for the first time in my life, and I liked it. Other than that, I tried to stay quiet. Mysterious.

A few times, Hannah invited a bunch of us to her big, shiny house. Girls *and* boys, which made me nervous, so I talked even less than usual. We watched movies on her enormous flat screen and ordered pizza with fancy toppings, and I tried to disappear into the huge pillows on the velvety brown sofa. I never invited anyone back to Gran's. There was too much I didn't want anyone to know.

Mostly, each day after school, I'd walk home. Then I'd get a snack and do my homework right away at the kitchen table. Lew always climbed up beside me to scribble with crayons. He said he was doing his homework too. He had to get up on his knees to reach the table. When we were done, we'd watch TV together in the living room. He'd curl up with his blanket, and we'd stare at the baby shows I secretly still liked to watch. Sometimes he'd fall asleep against my arm—a warm bundle. He made snuffling noises when he breathed.

Once in a while, Gran met me at school as a surprise, with Lew in his stroller. Those days we'd get cocoa or something on the way home. We'd stop at the playground, and he'd play with other little kids while Gran and I watched from the swings.

If it wasn't normal, I had to admit it was okay. Gran

was nice and school was pretty fun, and Lew was cuddlier than usual. I liked walking everywhere, and I liked the coffee shops near the house, and the playgrounds. If we had been visiting for any other reason, it would have been great.

And if Dad had been there.

Sometimes, when Mom wasn't at work or sleeping, she went out in the car, wearing high heels and a skirt, which wasn't usual for her. I was *not* about to ask her where she went. She was living her life and I was living mine. She didn't seem to care what I wanted or thought. Maybe she just went for walks in her high heels, and maybe she saw old friends from when she was a kid in Atlanta. Maybe she wandered around Target aimlessly in the evening, eating chips from an open bag she hadn't paid for yet. That was something she did that drove me nuts. Still, she was usually home to make dinner. Gran said Mom was getting herself together, "taking some space." I couldn't tell from the way she said it whether Gran thought that was okay or not.

Every night I'd call my dad, but I had to use Gran's phone, since the phone I'd gotten from the bread box worked for only a few days, even after I wished for a charger. I tried again with a second phone, but I guess you can't wish for an account with Sprint or AT&T or anything. I guess the bread box couldn't arrange that for me, which was too bad.

About half the time when I called, Dad was home. I was curious about what he was doing the nights he was out, but I didn't ask him any more than I asked Mom. Dad told you what he wanted you to know. Usually he'd just ask what I was studying in school. He never said anything else about the teaching job, and we didn't talk about Mom. I didn't tell him nice things about Atlanta, because I didn't want him to feel sad. There wasn't a whole lot to chat about, but it was always good to hear his voice.

I did call Mary Kate a few times too, but it was weird. One time she said I sounded funny and asked if I was okay, and I didn't know how to answer her. I really wasn't okay, but at the same time, I *was* okay. I didn't know how to explain that. She was so far away, and it's hard to tell someone about something they can't even begin to imagine. Even when they're supposed to be your best friend.

Mary Kate was at home, in *our* home. She was seeing *my* dad. She was sitting at the same desk in the same school in the same city as always. And I . . . wasn't. So I could say "I'm lonely" or "It's fun here," but she wouldn't know what I meant, not really . . . especially when both statements felt completely true and totally inadequate. I didn't understand it myself, and I didn't want her to feel sorry for me. It was too hard. I stopped returning her calls.

Mostly from then on I got email forwards from her on the computer in Gran's office, about cute kittens and bad luck. I couldn't help thinking they were dumb, though thinking that made me feel bad. She was still my best friend, after all. Occasionally she would send a picture of my house from her phone with a text that read "Miss ya!" or "See ya soon!" or something else like that. In one picture I could see my dad on the porch, sweeping. After that I stopped looking at the pictures. It was like I put Mary Kate in a box and set her on a shelf in my head or something.

In fact, it was a little like everything was a box. Gran's house was a box, school was a box, Dad was a box, Mom was a box, and the magic was a box. None of them seemed to know each other or to be part of each other anymore. My life was all in these little boxes, and I'd open one up and then close it again. Mary Kate's box felt smaller, like it had gotten shoved behind the other, bigger boxes. She was far away, something I didn't *have* to deal with, so I decided not to.

For sure I was homesick, but when things got really bad, I would go in my room and shut the door and wish. For books and lip gloss, but most often for food. Food made me feel better. I couldn't see the harbor, or the gulls, or my dad. But if I wanted to, I could *taste* home. Utz crab chips and Berger Cookies. Butterscotch Krimpets. Goldenberg's Peanut Chews. When I felt sad and bored and alone, I'd just pig out on junk food. I stashed the wrappers under my bed and waited to get fat.

Chapter 10

Then one afternoon—a few days after Thanksgiving, which we ate at a restaurant because Mom had had a late shift the night before and Gran said she didn't like touching dead birds—I came home from school to find Lew asleep on the couch, Mom gone, and Gran out in the backyard, digging in a dead flower bed. I could see her through the kitchen window. The house was cold.

So I turned on the TV in my room, patted the bread box gently, and made a wish. I'd gotten in the habit of patting the box each time I made a wish. It felt like a way of saying please, and maybe also thank you.

"I wish for some gravy fries from Jimmy's Diner," I said.

Instantly the room filled with a thick, comforting smell.

Gravy fries are exactly what they sound like—French fries drowned in gravy, and they are, without a doubt, the best comfort food of all time, except for maybe macaroni and cheese. Sometimes when it was rainy and chilly, Dad and I went out on special gravy-fry dates. The fries need to be crispy enough not to get soggy, and the gravy has to be good, homemade stuff. You sprinkle a little pepper on them and yum! I never even knew that gravy fries were a Baltimore thing until I got to Atlanta, but you definitely can't get them in Georgia, not even in places that sell both fries *and* gravy. People just stare at you like you're nuts if you ask for them.

There I was, sitting in my room on the rug with a hot china bowl warming my lap, watching TV and licking brown gravy from my fingers, when Gran knocked on the door and shouted, "What *are* you eating in there? It smells incredible!"

I looked down at the white china bowl and then over at the plastic salt and pepper shakers beside it. I stared at the metal fork. It was all so obviously from a diner, and there was no diner nearby. I hadn't even thought to wish for takeout so I could pretend to have gotten it somewhere near school. There was simply no way I could explain how I happened to have a china bowl of hot fries and a metal fork from a diner. I hadn't thought of how the fries would smell! I didn't have any idea what to do, so I pushed it all under the bed as the door opened, nearly sloshing gravy on the rug. Then I turned around and looked up at her.

"Rebecca?" Gran's face appeared around the edge of the door. "What's up?"

"Nothing," I said. "I'm not eating anything. Just watching TV." I licked the salty corner of my mouth.

Gran eyed me suspiciously. "That so?"

I nodded.

"Nice TV," she said.

"Um . . . thanks," I said. I figured the less I said, the less likely I was to screw up.

"You're welcome," she said back.

Then, I guess because Gran is the best grandmother in the universe, she turned and left. I knew I hadn't fooled her, but she decided to leave me be, which gave me a little time to gobble the fries up as fast as I could. Then I didn't know what to do with the sticky china bowl. It seemed gross to leave it under the bed. Wrappers were bad enough, but gravy would mean roaches. I knew *that* from the time Mary Kate and I accidentally left half an egg roll under the couch back home.

When I heard Gran running a bubble bath about an hour later, I decided it was time to clean up my mess. I snuck out to the kitchen to get a big trash bag. Running back to my room, I dumped the bowl and napkins and fork and stuff into the bag. Then I got down on my knees and started pulling out all the old snack wrappers from my bed.

I was working fast, with my back to the door, so I didn't notice when the door opened. I turned around only when I heard a loud squeal. A Lew squeal.

Behind me, Lew was shaking from excitement. "Tandy Tates!" he yelled, running toward me. He grabbed at the wrapper in my hand. When he saw that it was empty, he looked up at me. His top lip disappeared into his lower lip, which pushed out and started to tremble.

"No more?" he said to me, about to cry. "No Tandy Tates?"

I shook my head and pulled the Kandy Kakes wrapper out of his hand. "All gone," I explained.

Then—it was the weirdest thing—instead of howling and yelling for a treat, he put his head against my neck, stuck his thumb in his mouth, and said, "Lew want doh home."

If he'd been yelling and pitching a fit, I could have ignored him. I would have bagged up the trash and taken it out to the can right away. But he wasn't being bratty; he was sad. He was homesick, like me. He just wanted to feel better too. He wasn't even three, and he felt exactly like I did. I realized I hadn't figured out anything he hadn't figured out. From the moment the lights had gone out in our row house to right now, the only real difference between us was that he had a blanket.

And I had a bread box.

I looked at him, and he looked up at me. I gave him a big hug and said, "Hang on."

As he watched me, I put the rest of the wrappers in the bag. After that I went over to the bread box, which was open. I closed the lid and whispered, "Kandy Kakes, please?"

I opened the box. When Lew saw what was in it, his eyes got big and his thumb fell out of his mouth. I couldn't tell if it was because he understood about the magic or simply because there were Kandy Kakes in his immediate future. Either way, it felt really nice to make someone so happy. It felt wide open and good. In that room, with Lew, for a minute, everyone had everything they wanted. He didn't even seem to mind that the Kandy Kakes were chocolate and not peanut butter. He just laughed, dropped his blanket, and reached out his fat little hand.

I sat there on the floor with my brother and laughed out loud. We munched those Kandy Kakes, and then we wished for more and we munched those too. Like we were Cookie Monsters or something. *Munch munch munch.* His face was a revolting, chocolaty, happy-making sight.

After he swallowed the last bite, he licked his hands and then looked up at me. "Fank you, Babecka," he said with a tiny bob of his head.

"You're welcome," I said.

"More?" he asked. Not demanding, just curious.

"Maybe," I said. "But only if you don't ever ever ever tell anyone about the box. Only if you keep this a secret with me, okay?"

He nodded. His eyes were huge. He didn't take them off the box, not even to look at me when he said, "Yup!"

I wished for a third package of Kandy Kakes, and asked myself whether Lew could really keep the secret.

Then I decided not to worry about it, and I wished for a Clifford stuffed doll. I wished for a new pack of crayons. I wished for a huge roll of paper like we had back at home. I wished until I thought Lew had everything he could possibly want in the world.

That was how I let Lew in on the magic.

When Gran got out of the bath, Lew and I were back in the kitchen, with the roll of paper spread out, drawing a picture of a lion together. I drew the outlines and Lew colored everything in. He drew a big purple scribble next to the lion. It looked like a ball of yarn.

"What's that?" I asked him.

"The lion's daddy," said Lew, as though the answer were obvious. As though I should have known. He changed colors and gave the daddy an orange scribble on top of what I guessed was the dad lion's head.

"What's that?" I asked.

Lew stared at it for a minute. "Dunno," he said, and went back to scribbling.

Watching Lew, I got to thinking about all the little things I'd been wishing for. Was there anything else I could get for him that would make him feel better? I hadn't really thought at all about Lew being homesick too. I'd been thinking about myself. He was so little. I'd just thought he was having fun with Gran.

But now I knew he wasn't. Now it felt like we were alone in a bubble *together,* in the same small room. Suddenly I felt less alone, but I was also mad at myself—for using the bread box to wish for all these dumb little things for all the strangers at school I didn't care about, when my baby brother was feeling sad.

I decided I wasn't going to wish for pointless things anymore. It seemed wasteful to me now. It was one thing to wish for a homesickness treat once in a while, when I really needed it, to make me feel better. But lip gloss? Pens dried out and candy got eaten. Even the diamond— what could I do with a diamond? I had all this magic, this actual magic, and what was I doing with it? What was I really getting out of it if I wasn't making anything better?

More to the point—what did I really *want* to wish for? What did we really want? What did we need?

That night after dinner, alone in my room, I looked at the box. I thought about the wish I'd made for my mother's present. I thought about how the box had known what my mom wanted.

"I wish . . . for something that . . . ," I said slowly. "I wish for . . . *whatever* will make my parents get back together again."

I took a deep breath and opened the box.

It was empty.

CHAPTER 11

For the most part, I didn't touch the box for a few days after that. There was only one time, when my mom was missing her car keys and needed to run to the grocery store. She was in her room, rooting through the pockets of all the clothes in her dirty laundry basket and shouting, "I *know* they're here someplace. Otherwise how did we get *into* the house?"

I snuck into my room and whispered, "Mom's keys, please?"

I couldn't help feeling just a little smug when I joined Mom in her room and dropped the keys noisily on the floor beside her.

"Lose something?" I said.

She looked up at me from where she was kneeling next to the pile of clothes. Lew was beside her, playing with some dirty socks.

"Oh, thank God! Where did you find them?" she asked me.

Before I could answer, Lew looked up from beside her, smiled, and stuck his hand in the air, something he'd been learning to do at his preschool back home. He waited for me to call on him. "Oooh! Oooh!"

"What is it, Lew?" my mom asked him.

I held my breath. For a minute I was sure he was going to spill the beans, but then Lew put his arm down and blinked at me. I think he was probably trying to wink, but he can't do that, so instead he squeezed both eyes shut and laughed as he shouted, "Nuffing! Wight, Babecka?" He blinked again.

I let out a sigh of relief. I blinked both eyes back at Lew and said, "Right."

As I walked away, my mom called after me, "You still haven't told me where you found my keys!"

I kept walking.

Oddly enough, I found life was pretty much the same without the bread box. I went to school, where I mostly followed Hannah around, trying not to look too much like I was following Hannah around. I listened to Mr. Cook read poems out loud and did a bad job in gym class. I walked home each day. I did my homework. I ate dinner with my family and always offered to wash the dishes as soon as we were done. I kept on avoiding my mother for the most part, but that wasn't hard, because she wasn't around too much. She was working a lot.

The only real difference was that now, when I was alone in the afternoons, I wasn't *so* alone. Each day I spent a little more time with Lew, and *that* felt different. It was like he'd been a piece of furniture before, a big doll, and now he was a person, just because I'd noticed he was. Or maybe because he was in on my secret. Of course, I knew he didn't understand half of what I said to him, but what mattered was that I *said* things to him. I had someone to say things *to*. That made life easier at school too. I spent the day collecting little things to tell Lew about, saving up stories.

"Hannah says her favorite food is sushi, but I don't believe her," I'd tell him as we pushed and rolled blobs of Play-Doh around on the kitchen table. "I think she just tells people that to sound cool."

And Lew, who had no idea what sushi was, would hold up a smooshed red triangle and say, "Shooshee! Nom nom nom." He'd pretend to eat the Play-Doh, and then we'd laugh and laugh.

"Coleman is growing out his Mohawk," I'd tell Lew.

"Me too!" Lew would announce.

Or I'd read him one of the poems Mr. Cook handed out in class. Sometimes he'd listen to the words, the way he listened to lullabies at night, not exactly like he understood the words, but like he enjoyed them anyway.

Some days we went places, Lew and I. Half the time I pushed him in the stroller, and half the time he walked on his own. When he walked, I usually had to carry him at the end, but I got to like that, the feeling of having him on my hip. It felt like my hip was a little shelf. He was almost heavy enough to topple me over, but he never did. I could make it about three blocks before I'd have to put him down.

One day he climbed into his stroller and we walked and walked. We didn't stop walking for a long time, going farther than usual. Finally we found ourselves walking along a big, wide road, and then we crossed it and entered a cemetery. We read the gravestones, which were old and grown over. I stumbled upon the grave of the lady who wrote *Gone with the Wind*. Lew only wanted to knock on the doors of all the "little houses."

Another time we walked to the park to sit in the swings, but we didn't swing; we just sat together in a swing, me holding Lew on my lap. It was too cold for swinging, the wind sharp against our faces. We watched a man climb a tree in the park and put Christmas lights up. I realized that Hanukkah was coming too, though nobody had mentioned it at home. I wondered if I should send something to Dad. I didn't want to send him a gift and then have him not send me something. That would suck.

Once Lew and I walked all the way to a big baseball

stadium, which was strange to see empty. Cold and quiet and massive. We walked all the way around it. It reminded me of the Orioles games I used to go to with my dad, way up in the nosebleed section at Camden Yards.

"Do you remember going to see baseball with Daddy?" I asked Lew.

"No," said Lew.

Did he really not remember, or was he just saying no? Lew liked to say no. I hoped he hadn't really forgotten.

Just in case, as we walked home again, I tried to re-mind Lew about Dad. "He's kind of short, remember?" I said, peering over and into his stroller. Though as soon as I said it, I realized that Dad was probably very tall to Lew.

"Otay," said Lew.

"He's skinny," I said, "and he likes anchovy pizza. Fish pizza."

"Ew," said Lew.

I guess he remembered anchovies. That made me laugh. "He hums but he doesn't realize he's doing it until you tell him he is."

Lew started humming, and I wondered if any of this mattered. None of that would add up to Dad for Lew, if he'd already started to forget. Dad would just sound like some guy, some noisy, short, skinny guy who liked fishy pizza. That wasn't Dad any more than home was just boarded-up row houses and seagulls and snowball stands.

All of those things were just words. When I tried to think of words that meant anything, they just sounded like words. They didn't sound like the smells and the memories and the weather and the people and the day after day after day of living in a place. I couldn't explain *home*. Thinking about that, pushing the stroller along, I thought about what it might feel like to be a writer, a poet. To be able to use words the right way, the best way, so people could *see* what you were saying. The way the poems Mr. Cook read out loud made me see things. I bet it felt cool.

Anyway, whether Lew understood or not, I think he liked that I was talking to him. I'm pretty sure he did.

Being with Lew made me feel like me. It made me wish I could just kind of fade back to being Rebecca. If Hannah forgot about me, I could stop trying to look bored when Mr. Cook read poems, and I wouldn't have to listen to people getting picked on. I wouldn't have to roll my eyes. Since I'd stopped bringing candy to school, and lip gloss and stuff, it had started to feel like that might happen anyway. Hannah wasn't passing me notes in class so much, and she usually sat next to somebody else at the lunch table.

Then, in the cafeteria one day, when I'd forgotten my lunch money and had nothing to eat, I was just sitting there, watching everyone else munch and sip and chew. Hannah reached across the table and handed me a bunch of her grapes. She said, not quite looking at me but more at the rest of the table, "Broke today, Becky? That's a change. Did your dad lose his job or something?" Then she laughed and added, "Just kidding!"

I sat there holding the grapes. I could tell it was about to be my turn to get picked on. My turn. I remembered back to my first day. I remembered how I hadn't said anything nice to Megan about her curly red hair, which was perfectly fine hair. I knew I couldn't expect anyone to be nice to me now.

I also knew what I was supposed to say next, as though I'd been handed a script. If I didn't want to get picked on, I was *supposed* to laugh confidently and say, "Of course not, you freak!" Or, if I preferred, I could just roll my eyes and mutter, "Ha-ha, very funny." That was how to escape the moment. That was what Becky would do.

But I wasn't Becky, not inside, and I couldn't help thinking, what if my dad *had* lost his job today? What if I really cared, like Megan had cared about her big, curly hair? What if I couldn't laugh?

I remembered how my dad had come home on the bus, the day of the wreck, after they'd towed his cab away. I remembered how grim the house had felt, how worried my parents had been. I remembered taking Lew to the playground without being asked, just to get him away and give my parents time to talk. It didn't seem like the kind of thing to joke about, not to me.

So I didn't roll my eyes or laugh. Instead I did the opposite. I looked her dead in the eyes and said, "Actually, my dad's been out of work for a few months now, Hannah. And I don't even live with him anymore. I miss him, so it's not really very funny."

Hannah stared at me. The other girls eyed each other uncomfortably. I looked over at the boys' table and saw that they were watching too, that Coleman was staring. But I didn't care. I set the grapes back on the table, picked up my backpack, and turned away as fast as I could.

As I left the table, making sure not to stumble, I heard Hannah whisper, "Sensitive much?" A few of the other girls tittered for her benefit, but I was pretty sure I'd won whatever game it was we were playing.

I headed out the heavy metal cafeteria door to the bright, cold sunlight and the empty concrete of the school-yard. I sat down on a bench, alone, took in deep breaths of cold air, and raised my face up to the warm sun. I was proud of myself, but I was nervous too, so I waited for a minute after the bell before I went back inside. I'd rather wait for the safety of my assigned seat and Mr. Cook's poems. Then I'd go home and tell Lew what I'd done. He wouldn't understand, but he'd listen. He'd probably laugh and poke me or hand me a race car or a plastic frog or some other junk. Still, that would be something. Maybe I'd even tell Gran about this. This seemed like something she'd want to hear about, a story she'd like. Then, tomorrow, I'd start all over, as Rebecca Shapiro, the bookish kid who liked poems and didn't have to pretend otherwise.

As the day wore on, I felt less sure that I'd won. Hannah didn't just ignore me; she stared at me meanly, from under the long bangs of her perfectly layered hair. The other girls kept their distance in the hallway. Nobody came over to talk to me at my locker, not *anyone*. Not even the really nerdy kids were making eye contact with me. I guess that was fair, since I'd never talked to them either. As I was leaving the building, Maya bumped into me in the hallway. It didn't seem like an accident. When Cat did the same exact thing going down the steps, and then laughed, I was sure it wasn't.

Walking home, telling Gran didn't seem like a fun idea anymore. In fact, I was a little scared. I didn't even tell Lew. I just sat in the living room with him and watched the first twenty minutes or so of a movie about the last robot on a planet covered in garbage. A robot whose only friend was a cockroach. It was a good movie, a sad movie, but it didn't make me feel any better. That poor rusty little guy. I got up and left the room.

The next day was even worse. I didn't talk to anybody, from the moment I got to school until the moment I left. It's a weird feeling, not talking at all. I'd spent almost a month now not talking much, but when you really don't ever open your mouth, you start to feel weird. Your mouth gets to feeling pasty and thick. You get angry, and it starts to feel like everyone is staring at you.

When I tried to take my lunch into the library, Mrs.

Jenkins, the librarian, pointed me right back to the cafeteria, where I had to sit entirely alone at a table by myself, for everyone to see. I felt like I was in a cage or something, at the zoo. Not like a panda or a monkey, hanging out in a big glass box with all its friends, but more like something scaly and toothy and cold, like a crocodile maybe. Something that has to be kept apart.

I wasn't sure how I'd handle this, how I could stand to come back the next day. And the next. Again and again. It was too hard.

At the very end of the day, when I passed Megan in the hall, she handed me a note and smiled slightly. I was too surprised to even smile back. I felt like I'd forgotten how to smile. It had been a very long day of nothing but *mean,* and now . . . a smile.

She was gone before I knew what was happening. Standing there, with all the other kids I didn't know rushing past me loudly, I unfolded the note. I found a smiley face beside words that read, "Everyone will forget about it. They always do. Chin up."

Megan is different, I thought. *Megan is nice.* Then it dawned on me: *Maybe I can be real friends with Megan.*

The problem was, no matter how nice she was, Megan wasn't going to come sit at my empty table with me. In order to be friends with Megan, I'd have to go crawling back to Hannah. Could I stand it? Was it even possible now? I sighed.

Walking home, I remembered Megan's smile. I tried to think of some ways to hurry up the crawling back. I tried to think of painless ways to make up with Hannah faster. Maybe I needed to apologize, or maybe I needed to start up with the presents again. Maybe I just needed to be cooler. Even more *Becky*.

That was horrible to consider.

When I got to Gran's, I skipped checking in with Lew and made a beeline for my room. Carefully I closed the door, and then I stood in front of the bread box for the first time in almost a week. I stood there, wondering what might make me popular again. I asked myself, what was the awesomest thing I could think of? What would make people think I was *cool*?

Then I had a thought. I patted the bread box and said, "I . . . I want a jacket just like Hannah's."

The box would know which one.

Hannah's jacket was special. It was her most favorite item of clothing. Her "signature item," she called it. As she'd explained to me several times, it was a riding coat, and it was made of soft tan leather, the color of caramel, but it had red flowers stitched on it in a kind of country-western style that wasn't too country-western. Everyone loved Hannah's jacket.

She didn't keep it in her locker but carried it with her through the day, hanging it on the back of her chair in each class. She was extra careful with it, always dusting it off when there wasn't any dust on it. It wasn't a seventh-grade kind of jacket. It was an older-sister kind of jacket, or maybe even a college-kid jacket.

I opened up the bread box. There *was* a jacket just like Hannah's, exactly like Hannah's, folded neatly. I pulled it out and slipped it on. It fit perfectly. Like it had been made for me, which probably it had been.

I turned to admire myself in the mirror. The sleeves touched my palms. The lines of the coat hugged my shoulders. It felt rich—thin but heavy.

I pushed my hair aside with my hand so that the front swooped into pretend bangs. I didn't look like myself at all, I thought, with my hair that way. Mary Kate would barely recognize me if I went home looking like this. I looked better than me, older than me. I got butterflies staring in the mirror. Maybe it wasn't all bad to be cool. I patted the bread box again and wished for a headband. I fixed my hair so that the swoop stayed.

I made another wish and filled my pockets with the Starbucks gift cards from the bread box.

CHAPTER 12

The next morning, after watching Lew arrange raisins in a circle on top of his oatmeal and feeling a little bad that I hadn't played with him the day before and that I didn't have time for him now, I locked myself in the bathroom. I got dressed very, very carefully. I pulled on my skinny jeans and slipped into new red ballet flats. I picked out my favorite black shirt. Then I did my hair in the swoopy new way. When everything looked perfect, I went to my bedroom and put the jacket on. It all felt just right.

I picked up my backpack, ran down the hallway, and shot out the front door, shouting, "Off to school!" before my mom or Gran could catch a glimpse of me. I knew the jacket was too much. I knew they'd ask questions if they saw it.

I also knew I looked really good. Each time I caught

a glimpse of myself reflected in a car window, I couldn't help smiling. I felt pretty. I knew where I was going. I didn't feel like *Becky,* exactly. I felt like someone else. Maybe someone older. Or someone richer. Or *something.* I wasn't sure. I felt *new* in my jacket, and I was pretty certain that, just like Megan had said, soon everyone would forget about what had happened at the lunch table. They'd be too jealous to ignore me, too impressed to make fun. I figured I'd begin with Megan. I'd get myself an ally.

Before I could say hello to *anyone,* before I could even make it inside the doors of the school, *they* saw me. Or I should say, they saw the jacket.

"Oh. My. *God!*" Maya called out when I neared the front steps. She was standing, facing me, in a tight little circle with a few other girls. When she spoke, the circle opened and turned to see what she was talking about.

"Hi," I said, walking over like there was no reason I shouldn't walk over to them, like there was nothing wrong at all, like they hadn't spent the last two days treating me like garbage. I walked over, even though the tone of her voice made me feel uneasy.

"Look at you!" Maya said. "How did you manage *that?*"

"Hannah lent it to you?" asked Megan. "Maybe because she felt bad about . . . the other day?" She looked at me hopefully.

"No," I said, setting down my backpack and taking a

deep breath. "Nope. Actually, this is mine. *My* jacket. I just got it." I brushed an imaginary fleck of dirt off the lapel.

"Really?" Cat asked. I couldn't quite read the expression on her face. It was like . . . like she knew a secret. "Where'd you get it?"

"Oh, you know . . . ," I said, thinking fast and deciding to lie vaguely. "Online."

"Where online?" asked a girl I'd never really talked to, an eighth grader named Maddie.

"Um. I don't remember."

"That's funny," added Maddie. "Because I'm pretty sure Hannah said that hers was one of a kind, handmade, but maybe it isn't!" She snickered. I couldn't decide if the snicker was aimed at me or at Hannah.

"She . . . she did?" I asked.

"Yeah," said Maya. "She said it was a designer thing her dad had gotten made for her. She made a big deal about it being from, like, Paris or somewhere. I forget. London?"

"Italy," said Cat. She turned back to me. "Her dad went to Milan. Remember?"

"No, I—I don't remember," I stammered. If only I had—

"That's funny," said Maya. "She talks about it enough, but anyway, maybe yours is just a knockoff or something?"

"Um, yeah, maybe—that must be it," I said. I nodded in what I hoped was a casual way. I was sweating under the jacket. I felt chilly and hot all at once. I wished I could run home and climb back into bed, start the day over. It was way too late for that now. "It probably is—what you said—a rip-off."

"*Knock*off," said Maddie, "not *rip*-off." She laughed.

"*Knock*off, knockoff . . . ," I repeated, looking down at my feet. The toes of my ballet flats were newly scuffed, and they looked too red to me now. Like maraschino cherries. They looked like toy shoes. "It's just a knockoff."

I breathed deeply and prayed for this to be true. A knockoff didn't sound like a good thing to have, but it sounded way better than the alternative. What would Hannah do when I showed up with a coat *exactly* like her one-of-a-kind jacket? How would I explain that there were two one-of-a-kind coats in the same school? Could the bread box even do that? Could it have created an exact replica of something? Could the box *clone* something? I wondered what would happen if I wished for the *Mona Lisa*.

Then, for the very first time, I wondered just where, exactly, the things I wished for came from. How they managed to appear in the box the very moment I wanted them. But I didn't have long to think about it—

"Come on!" said Cat, picking up her bag and starting up the steps. "We'll be late, and now I can't wait to see Hannah." She gave me a mean smile.

I felt sick. I felt *so* sick.

"Come on, Becky," said Megan gently, hanging back for me. "It'll be okay. Who cares if your coat isn't a real Italian one like hers? Who cares about coats?"

Evidently a lot of people, I thought. Out loud I said, "Thanks."

I shuffled up the stairs behind the red pouf of Megan's hair and into school. I trudged through the sea of kids whose names I mostly still didn't know to what now felt like my doom.

When we got inside, there was Hannah, standing at her locker with her back to us. We walked up the hall toward her. I felt like I might puke. The jacket was weighing on my shoulders, pulling me down.

"Hey, Hannah!" Cat called out eagerly. *"Hannah!"*

Hannah whipped around, her hair fanning out, her eyes wide open. She began to say, "Guess what! Someone stole my—" Then she took everything in—she saw *me*.

She stopped speaking.

She closed her perfect mouth.

She looked me up and down.

She crossed her arms and smiled, suddenly much calmer.

"I was just saying," she said, "that someone stole my coat." She laughed. "What's up, Becky? Are you *someone* now?"

"No," I said, not thinking.

"You're *not* someone?" She smiled meanly. "I didn't think so."

"No. I mean, I didn't steal it. I—I—"

"What, you were only borrowing it?" she asked with a smirk.

"No, really. I bought it. Online."

"*Sure* you did," whispered Cat.

The other girls were enjoying this. I glanced over at Megan. She avoided making eye contact with me. She chewed her thumbnail and looked at her hand intently as she did it.

I squirmed. "No, but . . . well . . . maybe someone else stole it and posted it on eBay, and then I bought it without knowing," I said.

"I had it yesterday," said Hannah flatly.

"Maybe it's not the same coat!" I said, grasping at straws. I tried to keep my voice from rising or shaking. I didn't want to cry. I wouldn't be able to stand it if I cried now. "And it's just a coincidence that you got yours stolen when I happened to get mine."

"Unlikely," said Hannah. "Since mine was one of a kind. Mine was special."

"We told her that," Maya rushed to say, looking proud of herself.

"Yeah," said Cat. "We told her."

I felt like I might have a heart attack. Did twelve-year-olds have heart attacks?

The other girls backed away slightly as Hannah, still laughing, moved in on me to inspect the coat. She ran her finger along the red stitching. Then, with a quick jerk, she pulled the neck of the coat out and peered down at the tag.

I went limp. "It's not yours!" I bleated, hoping against hope. "It's a knockoff."

Hannah stopped laughing.

"I didn't steal it—"

"Oh, Becky," said Hannah, her voice serious, cold, thin, and as sharp as a razor. "It's mine—look!"

The other girls craned their necks and bunched around me to see, like dogs in a pack. They all stared at the back of my neck. Then they all stepped away from me.

"You're a thief," said Hannah in that same steely voice, "and a liar, but at least now we know it. To think I almost felt bad for you yesterday. I *almost* apologized for saying that stuff about your dad."

Hannah jerked at the neck of the jacket, and I closed my eyes. The coat came off inside out, spilling those stupid plastic coffee cards everywhere. I heard them fall and hit the ground. When I opened my eyes again, I saw what everyone else had seen a minute before—her name, *Hannah Ross,* ironed neatly onto the tag by some mother who did things like that for her kid. Hannah's mother.

I looked around me. All the girls were smiling. Except Megan, who just looked surprised.

I ran, pushing my way down the hall, through crowds of kids who would never be my friends.

Behind me, someone yelled out, "Now I wonder where all that candy was coming from too!"

A second voice chimed, "Yeah!"

I pushed open a door and dashed into a stairwell, down into the basement, where nobody ever went. When I thought I heard footsteps on the stairs behind me, I turned a corner into a dark hallway. Quickly I grabbed for the first door I saw and threw myself inside. I looked around and saw that I was in a janitor's closet. I locked the door.

Then I sat down on an overturned bucket and waited silently.

I *wasn't* going to cry. I refused. I couldn't give someone like Hannah—someone so shallow, so horrible, so dumb— any more of me. I wouldn't waste my tears on her. I just sat in that tiny room, under those greenish fluorescent lights and surrounded by mops, and *felt* like crying.

I wasn't sure how long I could stand to sit there. It reminded me of that first day in Atlanta, in Gran's attic. How long could I go without doing anything?

I reached into my backpack for a pen and a notebook. At first I thought I might try to write a poem, but that just felt too . . . silly. I wasn't a poet, and I didn't have any idea how to write a poem, not a real one. In school back home, whenever we were supposed to write a poem for an assignment, I just made a list of words that sounded good together, words that were kind of emotional—dark, cold, rain, night, blah blah blah. I usually got an A, but the poems weren't very good, not really. I knew that. Especially not after hearing the poems in Mr. Cook's class.

Instead I decided to just write down everything that had happened, as best I could, because it was something to *do* and because I thought it might be a little like talking to someone—even if I was only talking to myself and a piece of paper. I wasn't trying to make it sound good. I was just trying to get it all down. All the things that had happened so far. I wrote about Mom, and Dad, and the night the power went out. I wrote about driving to Atlanta, and about Gran, and the bread box. I wrote about everything I'd wished for and about my walks with Lew. I wrote about Megan's poufy hair, about laughing at all Hannah's stupid, mean jokes, even when it felt wrong. I wrote about telling Hannah off. I wrote for hours in that funny closet that smelled like bleach, but then, when I got to the part about the jacket, I felt myself start to get all prickly and upset again.

I tried to push that down. I clenched the pen in my fingers and gritted my teeth and stared at my feet. I said under my breath, "She isn't worth it. No crying. Dad would never cry over someone like that."

I was *not* going to cry over her. I was going to keep writing. I took a deep breath and wrote down, "So what? I took a jacket. Big deal." I added, "It was an accident and I am not a thief."

But staring at what I'd just written, I began to think

about whether that was true. If the bread box had magically whisked the one-of-a-kind jacket away from Hannah's house, then where had all the *other* stuff come from? In fact, maybe I *was* a thief. The candy and the chips—maybe *everything* was stolen. I closed my notebook, chewed my pen, and thought. . . .

The fries *had* come from Jimmy's Diner, after all. I'd wished for them to be from Jimmy's specifically. Of course, I'd only been imagining they'd be exactly like Jimmy's fries. I hadn't meant to steal them from Jimmy himself, but maybe they'd flown right off the table under some poor guy's nose, just as he was about to take a bite. Was that what had happened?

Wow.

If that was true, I guessed the chips and cookies had been whisked to me from other places in Baltimore. I imagined Lew's Kandy Kakes flying off a rack in a 7-Eleven, right in front of some startled teenager who was reaching for them. I thought of a bag of chips, blinking out of sight at the Royal Farms.

Of course, the keys really *had* been my mom's, so they'd been taken from wherever Mom had left them. Why hadn't that occurred to me at the time? It wasn't like there were two identical sets of keys floating around the world, each with a worn leather tag that said OCEAN CITY, MD. The box had just retrieved them.

Then . . . what about the spoon? Mom had said it was

expensive. Who had I taken that from? I remembered it being cold. Where had it been the moment before I found it? Who were Adda and Harlan?

And what about the TV? Had I stolen a TV? The magnitude of what I'd been doing all these weeks hit me. Wow. I really was a thief! I was almost impressed with myself. Ashamed too, but wow.

Of *course* the phone hadn't worked for long, because whoever the number really belonged to had probably gotten a new one and canceled their service.

And the iPod filled with songs—whose was it? Who had picked all those songs carefully, only to have me take it?

At last I thought about the money, and I wanted to fall over. I had stolen a *thousand* dollars!

And a diamond! I was a diamond thief!

I didn't want to cry now, not at all, but I also didn't want to write anymore. I only wanted to run home and bash the bread box to pieces. Throw it into traffic to be hit by a truck. I *knew* not to steal. I knew I had to return everything. But how? How could I possibly do that? How could I make this right? How could I figure out where it had all come from? There was no way to know, was there?

I remembered all the crumpled ones and fives. Were they even all from the same place? Maybe they were from different places, from the pockets of people who really needed that money. Maybe they'd come from Gran! Had I stolen from Gran? I groaned out loud.

Too loud I guess, because right after that, I heard someone call out, "Who's in there?"

Moments later, someone was banging on the door. And when I opened it, a white-haired lady with a huge ring of keys, someone I'd never seen before, peered in. She asked me where I was supposed to be. When I didn't answer, she dragged me up to the main office, where Mrs. Cahalen gave a deep sigh as I walked through the door. Then she motioned me into a chair for a little talk about how everyone knew I was having a hard time but that I needed to try harder, for Gran's sake.

"You don't want to be a burden to Ruby, do you, dear? Not when she's opened her home to you?" Mrs. Cahalen raised her eyebrows at me and peered into my face.

I *didn't* want to be a burden, actually, but I also didn't think Gran would ever say that about me.

"Sorry," I said. "I'll try harder." I glanced over at the white-haired lady, who was still standing by the door to the office. Didn't she have anything better to do?

"Well," said Mrs. Cahalen with a sigh, "I *guess* we can give you one more chance without bothering your *poor* grandmother, or Principal Harding. As long as you promise to try . . ."

I did not like Mrs. Cahalen.

With an irritating glance at the white-haired lady, Mrs. Cahalen opened the door to her office. "Can you be sure that Becky makes it to Mrs. Hamill's class, please?"

Mrs. Hamill? Third period already? Had I been in the closet that long?

Perfect.

The next thing I knew, I was headed back down the hall with my arm clenched in the white-haired lady's skinny fingers. She had a mean grip.

The old lady opened the door on a roomful of kids with their heads bent over their desks, bent over the big unit test on mass and matter. She raised her eyebrows at Mrs. Hamill, who beckoned me in with a concerned look.

Hannah looked up from her paper as I slid into the seat beside her. She slitted her eyes and smiled as she whispered, "Thief."

I just looked down at my test. I stared hard, until the letters got all blurry, and I said to myself, *No crying, no crying, no crying.* It worked. After a while, the letters unblurred and I could read the first question. I took a deep breath.

1. To what Greek philosopher do we attribute the following sentence? "The sum total of all things was always such as it is now, and such it will ever remain."

I was starting to scribble "Epicurus" when the meaning of those words hit me.

I reread the sentence: "The sum total of all things was always such as it is now." I scanned farther down and saw the words "in a closed system, matter is neither created nor destroyed." I couldn't read any further. The letters swam and blurred as I thought about the magic, about the unicorn horn the box never gave me, and the keys it did. I thought about where everything had come from.

Of course I'd been stealing. I'd been stealing all along. Things couldn't be wished from thin air. *Of course, of course, of course.* We'd been talking about it this whole time, in school of all places. I just hadn't been paying attention. The more I thought about it, the crazier I felt. Everything was coming undone inside and outside me. So I decided to stop thinking altogether and concentrated instead on simply trying not to scream. I stared out the window and left the whole test blank. It didn't matter anyway. It was just a stupid test some girl named Becky was taking in a school she didn't really go to that was full of people who hated her, because she really was a thief and she deserved it.

When the bell rang, I flew out of that room. I flew out of the building. For the first time in my life, I cut school. I didn't think twice about it. I was never going back, not ever. I didn't care what my mom said. Becky was gone, and Rebecca was lost, and nothing made good sense because nothing made sense at all.

Chapter 13

I bolted out into the chilly day, down the steps of the school. I ran and ran, barely glancing around me for traffic, just staring at my feet, flashing in a red blur above the cracked sidewalks. I ran away from the school, away from the house. I ran along a hilly street, past the park with the zoo in it and along a bridge that crossed a highway. I stopped on the bridge for a minute and pressed my face and hands against the chain-link fence that was there to keep people from jumping. The metal was cold against my cheeks. Below me, the highway rushed loud like waves crashing. It sounded strangely like the ocean, like home.

A woman walked past me and gave me a concerned look, so I started running again, through intersections. Somewhere along the way, I lost my headband. When I finally stopped, to bend over double and take a deep, painful breath, I looked up and found I was in front of a deserted gas station, staring across four lanes of traffic at the wall that surrounded the old cemetery. Where I'd walked that day with Lew in his stroller.

I wished I had Lew with me now.

No, I didn't. I wished I were home with Lew. *Home* home. And I wished that none of this had ever happened: not the box or Mom and Dad fighting or Atlanta or Hannah or any of it. But that was one wish I couldn't even steal.

A few feet away, on the bench in the old gas station, a man was asleep under a dirty blanket for everyone to see. Surrounded by shopping carts of dirty clothes and aluminum cans. I thought about how tired he must be, to sleep like that, in public. I guess people get to a point where they don't care what anyone else thinks of them. I almost wished I could feel like that.

I didn't have anywhere else to go, and I figured the cemetery was as good a place as any to waste time, so I crossed the street and climbed over the brick wall. Then I wandered around for a while, staring at the old names and the overgrown plots, picking up trash and stuffing it into a torn McDonald's bag I found on the ground. The wind was biting, and I didn't have a jacket on; plus there was a lot more trash than I could stuff into the bag. What good was it doing? I stopped trying to pick up the graveyard and sat in the doorway of a mausoleum— one of Lew's "little houses." The stone floor was frigid through my jeans, but at least I was out of the wind. I pulled up my knees and hugged myself, shivering.

I tried not to think of all the dead people, or of the jacket, or of Baltimore, or of my dad. I realized I had a lot of things to *not* think about. But the thoughts that kept coming back, the ones I couldn't shove away, were questions: How could I possibly *fix* any of this? How could I return what I'd taken? I wanted to feel clean again. I wanted to undo what I'd done. As bad as it had been to be in Atlanta without Dad, it was even worse to be in Atlanta without Dad and feel like a dirty, rotten thief—a dirty, rotten, freezing, lonely thief who couldn't tell anyone what she'd done.

I couldn't go anywhere warm, not to the library or to the coffee shop, because I was so obviously twelve years old and supposed to be in school. Kids are never invisible during the day. Everyone knows if you're alone and you're not at school, you're cutting. I couldn't go home because Gran—and Mom if she was around—would want to know why I was back home in the middle of the day. So I sat there, shivering and thinking about how much my life had changed in a month. What would my old self in Baltimore make of where I was today? I didn't think she'd believe it.

Then something weird happened. I was just sitting there, cold and awful, stuck and lonely, when I heard a flapping of wings above me, on the roof of the mausoleum. I didn't pay too much attention at first, because I was absorbed in feeling crappy. Until, over the sound of my own teeth chattering, I heard a *skrreeee!* I jumped up and spun around. Sure enough, there on the roof of the little stone building sat a seagull, just one.

I didn't know if it was one of *my* gulls or if it was some other lost bird, but I felt a little better when I saw it, a little less alone. I looked at those ugly, beady eyes just a few feet above my head and remembered a line from English class. One of Mr. Cook's poems had somehow stuck in my head.

"Hope is the thing with feathers," I said out loud.

The gull, apparently, didn't care about poetry, because it flew off. But somehow, the words made me feel better. So I said them again, louder. "Hope is the thing with feathers." It felt good to say something out loud.

Then I sneezed, and that made me realize how badly my nose was running.

"This is stupid," I said to the graveyard, as though the dead people were listening, bored in their coffins. "I don't have to sit here like this. I *don't*. Even if I am a thief."

So I headed home, walking now instead of running, and thought about how nothing *here* mattered, none of it. Not Hannah, not the other silly girls at the lunch table, not even Megan. Not the test and not Mrs. Hamill. That school wasn't my school. This life wasn't my life. I could walk away from the bread box, and nobody would ever know a thing about what I'd done, except me. I could walk away from the school, and Becky too. Anyway, we'd eventually go home to Baltimore. Wouldn't we? It was taking a long time, but we *would* go back in the end. One way or another. Then all of this would lift out of my story, and I'd be okay again. Myself again.

If I got in trouble at home . . . Well, if I got in trouble, I got in trouble. It didn't matter. What was the very worst Mom could do to me? So all the way home I planned to tell my mom I refused to go back. I was done with lying. Instead I would simply inform her that I'd left school, and I didn't care what she thought about it.

"I *will* go to school, to *my* school, at home, just as soon as you can get me there!" I rehearsed the words under my breath.

When I walked through the front door, I found them all in the living room, playing Chutes and Ladders. Mom was there, drinking coffee in her scrubs, and right away she asked me, "What are *you* doing home so early?"

I lost my nerve. I stood there, all sniffly and cold, with my teeth chattering, and I didn't have the energy for a fight. I didn't want to argue today. It had been a bad-enough day. I just wanted to be home.

"Um, I'm sick," I said, without meaning to. "They sent me home." I didn't mean to lie. It just kind of popped out.

"Really?" asked Gran, looking up from a seed catalogue. "*How* sick? What *kind* of sick?"

"Sick sick sick sick sick." Lew sang the word like a nursery rhyme.

"Just . . . sick. You know, like a bad cold," I said.

I knew it was a pretty weak lie, but it was too late to change my story. So I coughed as loud as I could. I was almost certain I could throw up if I needed to. Just from feeling miserable.

"Why didn't they call us?" asked my mom, setting down her coffee. "To come and bring you home? What kind of school lets a kid just leave like that?"

"It's only four blocks," I argued lamely. "It was easier to walk."

"That so?" Mom answered me, chewing her lip. I could tell she didn't believe me, but she surprised me. She said, "Well, get into bed, and I'll be in to see you in a minute."

With an extra cough, I headed for my room.

Behind me I heard Gran say, "Well, now, *that's* a load of bunk if I ever heard it!"

Mom answered her, "Of course it is, but let's let it go this once. She's got a lot going on right now. And I'm hardly worried about Rebecca becoming a juvenile delinquent. She's not that kind of kid."

With a sigh, I climbed into bed and turned over, thinking that my pillow was the warmest thing I'd ever felt in my life. I also wondered if there were any other diamond thieves who were so misunderstood. I wondered how, exactly, you knew a juvenile delinquent when you saw one. I wondered just what kind of a kid I really was. Then I wondered what everyone was saying about me at school. I could just imagine Hannah's sneer. After that I wondered when the school would call, and I started to get scared. Now that I'd lied, I didn't want to get caught.

And this may be the worst thing I did with the bread box, because when I did it, I knew better. It was just downright sneaky, but I did it anyway. Climbing out of bed, I went over to the bread box and whispered, "Gran's phone, please?" Her little black phone appeared in the box, with all those silly numbers taped to the back.

I turned it off and slipped it under my mattress.

That night, maybe as some kind of karmic punishment, I really got sick. I guess I caught a cold sitting in the windy graveyard. I even had a fever, but it wasn't so bad, really. Sometimes it's nice to be sick, to give up trying to function, to crawl into bed and be cared for a little. Nobody suggested I go to school the next morning, and Gran brought me chicken soup for lunch. Lew shared his crayons with me, and his gross blue blanket. He read me a story, holding the book upside down. *The Runaway Bunny*. In his version, the baby bunny actually got caught on the fishhook. Then it turned into a dinosaur.

Mom had to work during the day, but when she came home in the afternoon, she brought me a stack of library books. They all looked really great, just the kind of books I liked best. How had Mom done such a good job of picking them out? How could she be so smart about me in some ways and so dumb in others?

All day Friday I just lay there in bed, reading and drinking ginger ale. The whole time the bread box sat there on the table, and when I wasn't reading, I stared at it. I thought about how to try and return the things I'd taken. I thought that might make me feel better, to send everything back where it had come from. The only thing I could think of was to put everything in the box and say, "I wish you would all go back to wherever you came from!" When I tried that, nothing happened.

That night, just as I was drifting off to sleep, a thought struck me. "Adda and Harlan!" I said, sitting up in the dark room. "Who are Adda and Harlan?"

I would probably never find the owners of the crumpled dollar bills, but the spoon . . . I snuck out of my room and into the den, where Gran had her desk. I turned on the computer in the darkness and Googled "Adda and Harlan." There was only one entry—one single entry in the whole entire world. At last, some luck!

I sat there at Gran's big rolltop desk, staring at the glowing screen, and felt giddy, and thankful that "Adda and Harlan" weren't "Betty and Joe." I pulled a sheet of paper from the trash and tore off a tiny piece. On it I wrote in my smallest handwriting:

Adda and Harlan Tompkins
4561 Camellia Drive
Clarkston, GA 30021

I folded up the tiny bit of paper and put it in my locket.

On Saturday I was miraculously better. I woke up to the sun shining through my window and felt great. I put on my clothes, brushed my hair, and went into the kitchen for breakfast, like everything was normal.

"Guess what!" I said, reaching for a cereal bowl. "I feel better!"

"Well," said Gran. "Isn't *that* just the funniest thing, how a body always feels better on the weekend!"

I pretended not to hear her and took my Cheerios into the living room. Lew followed me. We watched *Mary Poppins* under a blanket, even though I'd seen it a million times before. Lew hadn't, and it was nice, sitting on the couch together, laughing. It was how Saturday mornings are supposed to be.

CHAPTER 14

Later that day, I offered to take Lew for a walk. It was still cold, but I was itching to do something after my day in bed. I bundled up and walked fast to keep warm, pushing Lew's stroller quickly along the uneven sidewalks of the neighborhood. I didn't think about much of anything. My face was crammed down into my scarf, and my breath made the inside of it all hot and wet. That made me think that maybe mufflers are called mufflers because they muffle anything you might want to say. I felt nicely muffled. Lew stared at everything we passed from under a hat of Gran's that was way too big for him.

We walked past the park and the zoo, south to where the houses got smaller and uglier. The dogs we passed had scars and no collars, and their fur was reddish from lying in the Georgia clay. We walked past vacant lots overgrown with viny green plants. As we passed a bus stop with an overflowing trash can, a skinny lady came up, with bare legs in that winter weather, and asked us for a dollar.

For a minute I thought about handing her a thousand dollars and a diamond, but then I got scared and shook my head. "I . . . I don't have any money," I said, then turned the stroller around and headed back the way I'd come, almost running.

I was lost in my thoughts, mostly thinking about the bread box, trying to decide if the box was altogether bad. I was pretty sure there was nothing wrong with finding my mom's keys for her when she lost them. But I knew I couldn't use the box to get stuff I wanted anymore. I couldn't pretend I didn't know how the box got things for me.

While I was doing all this thinking, Lew was staring at everything we passed with a glazed expression. He looked cold.

"You cold? You want cocoa?" I asked him.

"Ess," I heard. Lew looked up at me, upside down in the stroller. My hair was falling in his face, and he giggled.

So I pushed the stroller into an unfamiliar coffee shop, unbundled us both, and ordered two hot chocolates from the tired-looking girl working behind the counter. She wore her blond hair in two braids that looked like she'd slept in them. They were all lopsided and messy. I won-dered why she didn't take a minute and brush her hair. It wasn't like she was working very much, since the place was basically empty.

As soon as I paid for our drinks, the waitress sat down and started reading a big book with a highlighter in her hand. She looked like she was studying hard. She stared down at her book and chewed the end of her pen. She looked pretty stressed out.

Lew and I went to the back of the coffee shop, where we climbed up onto the best couch, snuggled together, and sipped our frothy hot chocolates. I thought about . . . well, all the things I had to think about. Lew thought about whatever Lew thinks about. Batman, probably, or puppies or something.

After a while I turned to him and said, "Lew, do you think it's wrong to steal?"

"Ess," he said, blowing into his drink so that it splattered a little onto his face. I wasn't sure if he understood what I'd asked him, but it didn't matter. I was mostly just thinking out loud.

"What if stealing got us back home, to Dad?" I asked, without thinking about it very carefully.

Lew turned around and dropped his drink. It hit the coffee table and splattered onto the floor. At the same time, he put his arms up to me and started to cry the way little kids cry, just full-on bawling suddenly. He leaned over and wiggled into my lap and lay there crying, with his head in the elbow of the arm that was holding my own steaming cup of cocoa. I couldn't move him without spilling my drink too, and his cocoa was spreading on the coffee table and the floor. I didn't know what to do. I couldn't put the cup down, and I was afraid I'd burn him. We were just a terrible mess, but I wanted to hug him, so I just leaned my head over so that it touched him, making sure not to tip my drink, and said, "Shhhhhhhh . . ." He fell asleep like that, all twisted around, facedown in my lap. I guess he was pretty cold and tired.

The whole time the mess was spreading, and the waitress was studying at the other end of the room, clearly trying to ignore us. I sat and waited for the situation to be something I could deal with, but it only got worse. Finally I put my cup down on the wet puddle of a table. I stood up from the soaked couch and placed Lew back into the stroller. I didn't even strap him in or wipe myself off; I just covered Lew with his coat and made a break for it, leaving the wet disaster behind me.

As I passed by the register, I thought of something and stopped. The girl with the messy braids wasn't looking when I reached into my backpack, which was hanging off the handles of the stroller, and grabbed all the money I had with me. I shoved the massive wad of bills into the tip jar, rubber band and all. I tipped all of it. A thousand dollars, give or take. It seemed crazy, but we were leaving a big mess behind for the girl with the braids to deal with, and I hoped maybe the money would make her a little less stressed out. With a quick glance over my shoulder, I pushed Lew out of the coffee shop and back into the cold.

Back on the street, with the money gone, I felt less worried, better. If I hadn't returned the money to its rightful owner, at least I'd given it to someone who might need it, and at least I didn't have to think about it any-more. I wished I'd thought of giving it away sooner.

Pushing Lew, who was still sound asleep, home up the hill, I thought that it might be nice to collapse and sleep like that. To have someone take care of me when I couldn't go any farther. To be carried and pushed along. I couldn't remember ever being that little.

The walk back felt like it took forever, but we didn't get lost, and I moved fast. By the time we neared the house, I was almost running. I was very cold and wet from the cocoa and ready to be home. My fingers were freezing. I dashed up the sidewalk to find Mom and Gran peeking out through the front window at us. Mom looked wor-ried, and I hoped it was just that we'd been gone so long and not that Gran had found her phone and gotten a mes-sage from the school.

Either way, I braced myself for a fight as I pulled the stroller slowly up the steps. If I was in trouble, I only needed to get through the yelling part and the crying part, and then I could apologize. After that I'd be grounded and things would be okay. I could go to sleep.

The door swung open, and there was silence on the other side. No yelling and no crying. Just silence. Mom held the door and motioned me in, back down the hallway to the kitchen.

"Lew's asleep," I said. I didn't explain that he'd fallen asleep late in the afternoon because he'd been crying so hard.

"I'll put him down," said my mom. "You're late. Wash up."

I did.

It was weird to eat dinner without Lew. In the whole month we'd been in Atlanta, I'd never had a meal with just Mom and Gran. It felt strangely grown up. I noticed Mom's eyes were red. She didn't eat her spaghetti but just ripped her bread up into little pieces and ate them slowly. I couldn't stop shaking my leg under the table. I didn't finish my spaghetti either.

Gran was acting funny too, a little too chatty—to make up for Mom, maybe. She talked for five straight minutes about lily bulbs she wanted to plant, as if Mom and I cared.

Right after dinner, Mom excused herself to disappear into her bedroom. When I passed by the door, it sounded like she was talking on the phone in a hushed voice. I put my ear to the old brass keyhole in the door. "No, don't," I heard her say. "Please don't. I'm not ready. It won't do any good. Not yet, anyway."

Was it possible that she was maybe, finally, talking to Dad? I almost hoped not. She didn't sound happy.

"I don't know," she added. "Maybe never. Don't push me."

I headed for my room, where I sat on the bed all tense and jittery, like a windup toy that's been wound too far. I felt ready to explode. I waited for my mom to come and explain what was going on. I waited for Gran to come and yammer at me about nothing. I just waited.

But after all that, nothing happened. Nobody showed up. I sat there trying to read another mystery, but the story kept drifting away from me. So I paced my room instead, listening to the house quiet down for the night. I felt like I was going crazy. Hours passed and Mom went to bed. I heard her door close. I saw the porch light blink off through my window. I heard Gran brushing her teeth and then watching TV in the living room, like she always did right before she went to sleep. It was infuriatingly normal, and it all made me worry. What was different? What was Mom so upset about? What was going on? Was she talking to Dad? What were they saying? It was driving me nuts! What did he want to do that she didn't want him to do? Why didn't anyone seem to remember that I was here? Nobody even came to say good night.

I heard the TV click off and the soft shuffle of Gran's slippers in the hallway. Still I waited another couple of minutes before I climbed out of my bed and tiptoed across the floor to stand in front of the bread box.

I tried to rethink all my wishes. I backtracked. I considered everything that had happened so far. Because now I knew just what the box *did,* and I knew that if I made a wish, if I chose to ask for anything at all, I *was* stealing. I was *choosing* to steal.

Even so, I knew there was one wish I was willing to make. No matter who I had to steal from to get it. No matter what. If I was going to get rid of the box, or destroy it, or abandon it, or whatever, there was *one* thing I had to try first. Because what else could I do?

Everything felt like it was closing in on me, shutting down. I couldn't go back to school. I wouldn't talk to my mom, and now it seemed like she didn't want to talk to me either. Mom, who had always talked and cried and shared too much, was shutting me out.

I had no friends, and Dad was far away, and although Gran was great, she was just Gran. She was for treats and presents and giggles, but not for real. Really, I only had Lew, and he was almost too little to be a person. Something had to change everything—had to change things fast. Something. Now or never. It was up to me. Even though the wish hadn't worked before, I had to try again. I had to believe that the magic could help me. I had to believe that *something* could.

So I wished.

I took a deep, nervous breath before I whispered softly at the box, "I wish for whatever will make my parents get back together." I gave the box an extra pat.

I waited before I opened the box. I felt shaky. I wanted it to work so badly. I *needed* it to work! My hand shook when I reached for the door. I squeezed my eyes shut.

And when I opened the box, and then my eyes . . .

The box was empty.

Of course it was.

There was no hope left. Nothing that would make them be together again. The box knew that, even if I didn't.

I snapped the box shut.

I wanted to scream.

Why had I thought it would work this time? How had I been so stupid? Nothing was any different. Nothing had changed at all. It was the same horrible wish, and it would be the same horrible wish forever. My wish would never change. Would I ever stop wishing it? Would I ever be okay with the way things were now? Would I ever *want* to be okay with it? That was maybe the scariest thought. That I could adjust, learn to be okay. That I might want to be happy anyway, without Dad.

I guessed I had to be nuts to try the same thing over and over, to stand there in the darkness and make the same wish again and again. I'd have to try something different, but what? What else could I wish for? I only wanted one thing.

Then something hit me, a thought I hadn't had before. A wish I could make that was a little different, but only a little.

I took another deep breath. I closed my eyes. This time I said, "I wish for something that *might* help my parents get back together."

I opened the box a crack, holding my breath.

Inside, something seemed to be glinting. This time the box wasn't empty!

A few twenty-dollar bills and a handful of loose change. More money? I didn't need money! I'd already given away more money than any kid my age had a right to. Money wouldn't tell me how to help my parents. I was just stealing again from some poor stranger. What could possibly be different about this money?

Then I reconsidered—this time the money meant something. This time the cash was a glimmer of hope. The box had not been empty, and the difference between "empty" and "not empty" was everything. This meant there *might* still be a chance, if I could figure it out. The box was trying. It was just confusing. *Might* made everything loose, open, hard to figure out. *Might* was a glimmer; it wasn't a promise, not really. *Might* was another kind of puzzle. I thought about that for a minute.

I wished again. I said, "I wish for something *else* that might help my parents get back together."

This time I got a phone charger.

But not just any charger. I laughed sadly when I saw it. It was Mom's. Of course. Mom was terrible about letting her phone run down, and it drove Dad crazy. They fought about it all the time. But what good would it do me? This was only any use to Mom. It was her charger, to her phone. I couldn't do anything with it.

I took out the charger and closed the box again. I crossed my fingers and said, "I wish for instructions to go with my phone charger. I don't know what to do with it."

When I opened the box, I didn't get instructions for how to get my parents back together. I only got instructions for the charger itself. A little booklet, in three languages. I could tell that at some point, long ago, Mom had stuffed the booklet into the junk drawer in the kitchen at home, because when I picked it up I caught a whiff of Juicy Fruit gum and glue sticks. I knew that smell. It made me sad. I dropped the booklet on the floor.

I wanted to wish again, but I felt thickheaded, like when I haven't studied for a test at all and have to randomly guess at the answer to a question, knowing I'll get it wrong but trying anyway because although it's unlikely I'll pick the right answer, it isn't actually impossible. The capital of Idaho *might* be Springfield.

At the same time, I had this sense that I was finally getting somewhere. I was learning—if I could only learn fast enough. Unfortunately, I was also getting tired. I decided to try one last time. "Isn't there anything that will get me home? Please?" I asked the bread box. I stood there looking at the box for a minute before I opened it.

When I opened the box this time, I found a bus ticket. To Baltimore. I had wished sloppily.

"That's not what I meant," I hissed at the box. "It isn't good enough. I meant that I want my parents back together. I want everything back the way it *was*! Can't you help me?"

The box just sat there, gaping at me, useless.

I was tired, incredibly tired of trying and failing at everything. I set Mom's charger on the dresser so I'd remember to sneak it back to her room in the morning, and then I tore up the bus ticket. I put the money in my backpack.

I got into bed and stared at the bread box from across the room.

Magic—big deal. What good was magic?

CHAPTER 15

The next morning, Mrs. Cahalen stopped by while she was out walking her dog. "Unofficially" and "off the record" and "just to be helpful" on a Sunday morning. She said she was popping in to say hello because Gran hadn't been answering her phone, and since the office didn't have a number for Mom, they hadn't been able to get in touch at all.

Mrs. Cahalen didn't just tell them I'd cut school. She stood there in the house and told them everything. She said that Hannah had generously come forward on Friday to "explain about the incident," because she felt "bad for Becky," who was having "such a hard time adjusting." Mrs. Cahalen, being a "good friend," wanted to check in with Gran—and Mom, naturally. Then, I guess, she took her dog and went home. Really, I don't care where she went.

I didn't see Mrs. Cahalen or the dog for myself. I was still sleeping when this all happened, but Mom came in and wrenched me out of bed. She marched me to the kitchen, still groggy and confused. She tossed me into a straight-backed chair and stood above me with tears in her eyes as she repeated everything Mrs. Cahalen had said.

At the end of all that, she said, "We are so disappointed in you, Rebecca. What's going on? How did this happen?"

At first, I was too asleep to process what she was saying. I just ran my tongue over my fuzzy, unbrushed teeth and tried to look like I was feeling really sorry, which I almost was. Her voice got more and more quivery, and at last she said, "Things are hard enough for me right now, Rebecca. I'm alone, on the edge—the *edge*. Do you understand? I don't need this. I can't believe this!" Her voice shook. "I have a lot on my mind right now. I am juggling so much and I am overworked and I just wanted a little time to think things out for myself. Everyone seems to need something from me or want something, and I don't even know what feels right or wrong anymore, and there are so many people to think about." She paused for a breath. "I don't want to have to worry about *you* too! You're usually so . . . so fine. Usually you're the one I don't have to worry about!"

I looked up at her. I forgot about my teeth. She didn't want to have to worry about me? I was just one more thing to deal with? Did she think this was all just happening to *her*? Did she really think she hadn't made this mess herself? Had she forgotten all about me and Lew? I wanted to stand up and yell at her, but I reminded myself that "less is more" and tried not to get upset. If I started trying to explain, I'd talk myself into a hole. I'd just look like a big baby.

So I sat on my hands and said, "I *am* fine. Don't worry about me."

Mom laughed in a weird, bitter way. "Don't worry? How am I supposed to manage that? You stole, Rebecca. That is *not* fine!"

I shrugged and bit the inside of my mouth to keep from saying any more.

"Don't you think you owe me a little more than that?" she asked.

I shrugged again.

"You are infuriating," said my mom, standing over me. "Talking to you is like talking to a . . . a wall. How can I help you if you won't talk to me?" Her voice was cracking again. Her hands were spread out in front of her, and her back was bent over so she could peer down into my face, like someone in a police show on TV.

I looked up into her eyes, but I still didn't answer her.

"How?" she said again. This time she just sounded defeated. "How. How. How." She was just repeating the word until it didn't sound like a question anymore. Then she seemed to give up and fell into the chair beside mine. She said, "*Please?* Please, help me understand, Rebecca? Can you?" She didn't sound mad anymore. More tired. "Look . . . I don't really care about Hannah's jacket, but what's wrong with *you*? On the inside. Are you okay? I'm worried. And when you don't talk to me, it's like . . . it's like I'm dealing with your dad all over again!"

I knew she was trying to make me feel bad, but it made me kind of proud. I'd rather be like Dad, if I got to choose. I looked down at my feet on the floor. I didn't know what there was to say.

Mom took a deep breath. "Okay, let's start over. You cut school," she said. Her forehead was all wrinkled, but she seemed to be done yelling at me.

I nodded.

"Honestly, we knew that already. We figured that part out. We were letting it slide. . . ."

I thought about thanking her, but it didn't seem like the right time, and anyway, she kept talking.

"But what on earth is this about you stealing a leather jacket? Since when are you a thief? And since when do you care that much about fancy jackets? Is this all a cry for attention? We're confused."

I shook my head.

I wanted to know who "we" was. Had she talked to Dad? Did Dad know what I'd done? I felt panicked at the thought.

I stared back at her. A teeny tiny part of me actually wanted to tell her what had happened, as crazy as it all was—about the magic and Becky and the money and everything else. But a bigger part of me didn't want to tell her anything. I wanted only one thing from my mom. "I don't . . . know," I said. "I just want to go home. I guess that's all there is. I guess I don't have anything else to say. I just want to go home."

Mom stared at me for a long, long time. It was like a standoff. I tried not to blink. I wondered what she was thinking.

When she finally opened her mouth, she said, "Can't you think about anyone but yourself?"

And that . . . I couldn't stand. Sitting there like that with her leaning over me, pelting me with those wrong words. As if *I* were the selfish one. As if *I* were the one doing pretty much whatever I wanted, even if it tore my family apart. As if *I* had made all this happen. I stood up and faced her. That was when I realized suddenly, staring into my mother's eyes . . .

I was as tall as she was.

"Can't *you*?" I asked as calmly as I could.

She might still have been able to make it better then. I would have let her. She could have apologized or hugged me. Right then and there, she could have listened and agreed to go back home. I wanted it all to be okay more than I wanted to win.

But Mom didn't apologize. Instead, in an angry, grown-up voice, she said, "I am in charge of this family, young lady, and *what I do, I do for you.* I only want what's best for *you*—"

Hearing those words, I didn't feel bad anymore. I felt justified. "That's a lie," I said. My voice was rising, and I couldn't help it. "Because what's best for me is home, and Dad. Anyone could tell you that, even Gran. But you don't care about that, not at all. You aren't thinking about me, or Lew. You're thinking about yourself, and what *you* want and what *you* need." I spat this last part in her face. I couldn't believe I was talking to her this way. I meant to keep my cool, stay calm, but I couldn't. I forgot about "less is more," and the words just flew from me like fire— and exploded into loud, angry sounds.

"Oh, Rebecca," said my mom. Then she sat down in the chair, slumping into it, and I was left standing above her.

I had hurt her, but I didn't care. I was full of being angry now. Once the meanness started, I couldn't stop it. "So what if I stole a jacket?" I said. "You're worse than that. You stole *us!*"

"Oh, *Rebecca,*" my mom said again. Now she was going to cry. She reached out her arms to me.

"I'm *not* going back to that place, that school," I said. "I'm going home. I'll run away. I'll take a bus. I'll live with Dad. I'd rather live with him than with you anyway."

My mother's face crumpled. I had gone too far. I could tell. We both had. She wasn't even crying. She was just sitting there.

"Mom?"

She buried her face in her hands and didn't move.

Somewhere off in the distance, a police siren wailed. Then it was gone.

"Mom?"

Silence. She just sat there in the kitchen, like she was sleeping in that chair, her face in her hands, swaying a little. It scared me.

"Mom?" I said one more time.

This time my mother stood up and walked past me, grabbed her keys off the counter, and walked back through the house. I heard her open the front door. I heard her march down the steps. Then she was gone.

Slowly I headed back through the house, looking for Gran and Lew, but the house was empty. They'd probably gone out for a walk when Mom and I started yelling. So I went back to the kitchen. Mom had left her phone on the counter when she stormed out. Suddenly I really needed to talk to Dad.

He picked up on the first ring.

"Hi, Dad?" I said with a flutter in my chest.

"Becks!" he said. "Been missing you. You okay? You don't sound like my girl."

"I don't *feel* like your girl," I said. "I feel . . . bad."

"Oh no," he said. "I wish I could be there. What's going on? What's wrong?"

"Nothing," I said. "Or . . . everything. It's just . . . I hate Mom."

He sighed. "No, monkey. You don't. I don't either. We love her like hell."

"*I* don't," I said. "Not anymore. She lies. She says she wants what's best for us, but she"—I choked—"she doesn't even care."

Dad took a second before he said, "She does, Becks. She's just upset. I know that in the end, she'll be ready to help me fix this. She'll make it right."

Wow, I thought. *She has him fooled.* He had no idea what was going on. Maybe he was just too far away to know. I guess I took too long thinking about it, because then Dad said, "Hey, Becks? I have to run. Sorry. I know this is a bad time, but I need to go. We'll talk real soon, okay? And I'll see you soon too. I promise. I'll see you *real* soon."

"Okay," I said, "I guess—"

The line went dead.

I felt blown out and hollow, like the painted shells on the bottom of the hermit crab cage in the gift shops on the boardwalk. The ones no crab is living in. I walked from room to room, wishing Lew and Gran would come home, but it was just me, alone, all by myself, in a silent house.

I went to my room and stood in front of the bread box.

"Please," I said. "Please? Please send me something,

anything, that might get me home to Dad. Please help me find a way home."

I opened the door: another bus ticket. I sighed. I knew now that the bread box couldn't give me anything to fix my parents, because I·hadn't broken them.

I looked at the ticket, and for a heartbeat I thought I could do that—go home by myself. But it was a long way, too far, and besides, I didn't think I could ever leave Lew behind.

CHAPTER 16

That was a lonely day—just me, by myself in that quiet house. Gran and Lew stayed gone, and I missed them. I would have called them to find out where they'd gone, but there was no way to do that, since I'd stolen Gran's phone. I reminded myself that I needed to return it. Now that Mrs. Cahalen had busted me, there was no reason not to give it back.

I watched hours of television, because I had no idea what else to do with myself. It was boring. I turned on Gran's computer, but there wasn't really anything I wanted to do with it. At lunchtime I made myself a turkey sandwich. That was about all there was to the day. No distractions. Plenty of time to feel bad about everything, plenty of time to feel worse.

Finally, around five o'clock, Gran and Lew came home. When I heard them, I went to my room and got Gran's phone from its hiding spot under the mattress. I walked into the kitchen and set it on the counter in front of her. There were grocery bags all over the place. It looked like she was going to make tacos for dinner. Lew was on the floor, drawing a picture on a paper bag with crayons.

"I found this," I said, pushing the phone toward her.

"Found it, huh?" She stared at me very steadily.

I couldn't lie anymore. "No, I took it," I said. "I'm sorry."

Gran seemed to think about that for a minute, while I waited for her to be mad. At last she put the phone in her pocket and said, "Rebecca, I thank you for the truth. In light of the fact that you're already in deep doo-doo, you can consider this misdemeanor forgotten. Okay?"

I nodded.

"You and your mom get everything sorted out?" she asked.

"No." I bent down and picked up an orange crayon that had rolled over to my feet. I started to pick the paper off it.

Gran sighed. "That's too bad." Then her tone changed, and without missing a beat, she asked, "Hey, how many tacos can you eat?"

"Three. Where'd you go all day?" I asked, watching her stir.

"You know, just some places. Errands. The mall. We walked around the greenhouses at the botanical garden."

"Oh," I said. "I didn't know there was a botanical garden. That sounds fun."

"It was fun," she said. "And there are a lot of things you don't know." Then she stopped talking, reached for a big knife, and started chopping onions. My eyes began to water.

I sat down on the floor next to Lew. "Hi, you," I said.

"Hi, Babecka," he said. "I dwawing a mast." He didn't look up from whatever he was drawing on his mask. It looked a little like a mustache and a little like a star. He unfolded the bag and put it over his head. I couldn't help smiling at him.

We ate dinner, just the three of us.

I was doing the dishes while Gran made herself a cup of tea when we heard the front door open. I glanced up. Gran looked over at me and said quietly, "Be. Good."

I nodded.

Mom stormed into the room, moving quickly. Her eyes were red-rimmed. She didn't actually look at me, but she said to the room in general, "*I* will be taking Rebecca to school tomorrow before I go to work. I am the head of this family, and there will be *no* discussion about it."

Gran said, "Yes, ma'am!"

I kept my eyes on the dishpan.

Mom picked up Lew and carried him off to take a bath, and I could hear them laughing in the bathroom together, all echoing and splashy, singing the rubber-ducky song. I guess she was okay in general. It was just me she was mad at.

The next morning I couldn't seem to get dressed. I woke up early and stared at my clothes, and nothing seemed like the right thing to wear. I could just imagine how this was going to go—Mom walking me into the school in person, holding my hand like a baby, marching me through the halls while everyone snickered behind my back. What was the right shirt for dying of embarrassment?

Eventually I settled on an old green sweater. It was a Rebecca sweater, not a Becky sweater. My dad had bought it for me at a yard sale last year. It made me feel better wearing something that had come from Dad. After I put it on, I pulled my locket outside the sweater so that it showed. I could imagine him saying, "Chin up, monkey!" I opened the locket and made sure that the scrap of paper was still inside.

In the bathroom, I brushed my teeth extra hard. I brushed my hair extra hard too, until it crackled. I washed my face with Ivory soap that stung my eyes, in the hottest water I could stand. Then I took a deep breath and marched down the hallway to the kitchen, where my mother was waiting for me.

"Ready?" she asked right away, though I obviously hadn't eaten breakfast yet.

"I'm hungry."

She handed me an apple. "Don't want to be late on your first day back," she snapped.

We stepped out onto the porch together, and I stomped down the stairs. So did Mom. When we got to the edge of the walk, there was a funny moment. Mom hesitated. She paused just a little too long.

"What?" I said, turning to look at her.

Her brow was creased and she said, "It's just . . . I don't know where the school *is*. Which way do we go?"

In all the weeks we'd been here, she'd never once walked me to school. That's how little attention she'd been paying to me. Now that I thought about it, I realized that Mom and I hadn't walked anywhere together since the day we went to the zoo.

For a minute I was tempted to take her on a wild-goose chase, head off in the wrong direction, but that would only make her mad and make me late. I'd have to walk in alone, after the bell, with my mom at my side, and that would be worse than getting there on time, when at least I could melt into the sea of bodies.

"This way," I grunted, and turned right to trudge the four blocks to the school. She followed close behind.

Mom surprised me again when we got to the corner across from the school. She hung back.

"Aren't you coming?" I asked her as meanly as I could.

"Won't that just make it worse?" she asked, looking genuinely concerned.

"Yes."

"Then I'll stay here," she said. "You go ahead." She nodded.

"But I thought the whole point was to——"

"The point was to make sure you *got* here, Rebecca. To make sure you didn't run off, that you faced the music. I'm not trying to punish you any more than I have to. I know you don't believe that, but it's true. I just didn't want you to run away from this."

That's a laugh, I thought, *coming from the queen of the runaways.* But I didn't say anything. I just stared at her.

She sighed and said, "Honey, I mean this in a good way. If you have apologies to make, you should make them. If you have apologies to accept, I suggest you accept them. If you're in the middle of a fight, finish it. Trust me—you'll feel better once you do."

Half of me could tell she meant well and wanted me to hear what she was saying. But half of me could only think what a huge hypocrite she was. I didn't say goodbye. I just crossed the street quickly and walked up the stairs. I didn't look back and I didn't look around. I kept my eyes on my feet and moved fast. No good could come of eye contact.

Someone called out "Becky," but I just kept going. I wasn't Becky anymore. Becky was gone. I went straight to class. I didn't stop at my locker. I kept my eyes down and my mouth shut and I just breathed, breathed. . . .

I made it through homeroom.

I made it through math.

Of course, I wondered the whole time if people were staring at me, if they were passing notes about me, but I didn't look up, not once. I didn't see any point. I just had to get through the day. I could—I realized—suffer through just about anything if I didn't look at anyone.

Then came Mrs. Hamill's science class. I ran through the halls to be there first, figuring if I could get to my seat before Hannah got to hers, I might be able to avoid the painful moment of walking past her perfect knees. I could just imagine having to ask her to move her bag so I could get past—our eyes locking, her mouth in a mean smile, her eyelashes aflutter.

I was the first one to class. I walked into the room and murmured something like "Sorry" to Mrs. Hamill as I made my way past her desk. I slid into my seat and opened my book. I pretended to read, but the words swam, so I just sat there staring at the unreadable page, waiting for Hannah.

Then Mrs. Hamill decided to leave the room, just as everyone else filed in, so there I was, without a teacher to protect me, when Hannah marched over and stood above my desk with her little flock all around her. Maya was there, and Cat too. I could feel them staring down at my head. I could tell who they were by their feet, and that bothered me—the realization that I'd cared enough about these people to memorize their shoes. I didn't see Megan's shoes in the circle. I tried not to think about what was happening. Instead I pictured Lew, because it was the only thing I could think of that I knew would make me feel better. Lew laughing. Lew with jelly on his nose.

It didn't work. I could barely breathe. I reached for my locket, clutched it like a charm.

They stood over my desk, and I stared at the dirty tile floor for what felt like ten minutes before Hannah spoke. "Here's the thing," she said with a smug laugh in her voice. "I'm not even pissed you stole my jacket, Becky. I could forgive you for that and still be your friend, if only . . ."

I jerked my head up to look at her, confused. She stopped talking and stared at me, like she was waiting for me to say something.

She thought I still wanted to be friends? It hadn't occurred to me she'd think that. As embarrassed as I was by everything that had happened, I didn't care in the least about her anymore. Hannah was such a small part of what was going on, such a tiny little part, but she didn't know that. She had no idea what was happening in my crazy life, and I was so far inside it that I hadn't thought about what it looked like from the outside.

"I guess I *am* sorry for stealing your jacket," I said. "I guess I *should* say I'm sorry. I wish it hadn't happened, anyway. Now can you leave me alone?"

"Well, the thing is . . . you just aren't *normal,* Becky."

Hannah shook her head, and her sheep shook their heads too. "You try really hard to be, but you aren't, are you?"

When she said that, I noticed that behind her back, Coleman rolled his eyes. And maybe because of that—because of the eye rolling, but maybe also just because everything felt so tense and insane—something happened that I never could have predicted.

I laughed! I laughed out loud, too loud, so that all around the classroom, people turned to look at me. The day before I would have been embarrassed, but I didn't care anymore. All my fear and embarrassment faded away, and I laughed and laughed.

Hannah looked confused.

"What? What *is* it?" she asked, smoothing her perfect hair down instinctively. "You weirdo."

I just kept laughing. I saw Mrs. Hamill step back into the room, and Hannah didn't even notice. I didn't even care or stop laughing until Mrs. Hamill said, "Hannah, Maya, Cat—take your seats, girls," and they all turned around, surprised, and slunk to their seats.

Hannah sat down beside me, carefully, and then she looked over at me in a sideways kind of way. She looked funny, less sure of herself without her flock. I was still giggling. "What *is* it?" she hissed when Mrs. Hamill turned back around to write on the board. "What's so funny?"

I didn't answer her. Less is more.

"You're insane, you know that?" she whispered again.

I just sat there, smiling to myself, and it was like everything was better for a little minute. I felt like if I never said another word, she'd be afraid of me forever, but the thing was, I didn't even want that, not any more than I wanted to be *normal,* whatever that was.

I was smiling because I'd figured something out.

"What is it?" she whispered one more time. "What?"

"It's just . . . ," I said. "I don't think you have any idea what *normal* really is, Hannah."

She stared at me through her glossy fall of hair. "*What* did you say?"

"It's true," I said. "I'm as normal as anyone. We're all normal, and we're all afraid of you, maybe because you're mean, and pretty, and you have fancy stuff. So we play along; we follow you like morons. But . . ."

"But what?" she hissed.

I looked her dead in the eye. "But just because we follow you doesn't mean we *like* you. Followers aren't the same as friends. I don't think you even know what a friend is, really."

When I said that, Hannah looked startled, like I'd slapped her in the face.

I didn't know I was going to say it until I said it, and I didn't expect her to be so upset, but I guess what I'd said was the truth, because I can't think of any other reason it would have bothered her so much. She looked like she might cry.

I guess I was louder than I meant to be too, because when I looked around right afterward, I saw that everyone else was staring at us. Except Mrs. Hamill, who was still scribbling on the board.

Hannah stood up, walked to the front of the room, and whispered something to Mrs. Hamill. Then she grabbed the hall pass and left the room. When I turned to look behind me at the back of the room, I saw Megan's mouth hanging wide open.

I settled back into my seat and returned to staring at my desk.

The rest of the day wasn't as bad as I'd expected it to be. I ate lunch alone, of course, and in gym we had to play volleyball, which I'm truly terrible at, but it was a normal kind of bad day at school. For the most part, nobody seemed to notice me very much. During sixth period, Coleman got in trouble for refusing to sing "Winter Wonderland," which we were all learning for the holiday show that was coming up in a few weeks. That was interesting.

"I know you're Jewish, Coleman, but it's not a Christmas song or a Christmas show," sighed Mrs. Ogundele, the choir instructor. "It's a *winter* song and a *holiday* show."

Coleman shook his head and sat back in his chair. "It doesn't feel like that to me," he said. "*Snowmen?* It feels like Christmas."

I knew exactly what Coleman meant, but I was

surprised. I hadn't known he was Jewish. I watched him pout in his chair and made a mental note to tell my dad about the whole thing. He'd think it was funny too.

The best part of the whole weird day was the poem Mr. Cook had written on the board when we got there, about a guy who couldn't read, and so kept a letter all his life without ever finding out what it said. It ended like this:

> *His uncle could have left the farm to him,*
> *Or his parents died before he sent them word,*
> *Or the dark girl changed and want him for beloved.*
> *Afraid and letter-proud, he keeps it with him.*
> *What would you call his feeling for the words*
> *That keep him rich and orphaned and beloved?*

I didn't understand the whole poem, but it seemed like maybe the guy liked the letter because since he couldn't read it, it *might* be anything at all. The unread letter in the poem reminded me a little bit of the scrap of paper in my locket—how it *might* be something wonderful or nothing at all. The poem made me think about how I liked having the address with me, because the spoon *might* be something I could still fix. Though if I kept it like the man kept the letter, I'd never know. . . .

At the end of the day, I headed home alone. I walked fast, strong. *Dad would be proud of me,* I thought, *if he could see me right now.* I hadn't cried or run away. I had only said what was true. I knew I could go back to school the next day and survive it again, even though I didn't want to.

Technically, I supposed everything was pretty much as awful as it had been before—with my mom and dad, and all the things I'd stolen, and not having any friends. A lot of things were still royally messed up, but making it through the day made something feel better *inside* me, made me feel like something had been lifted or freed.

As I was walking along, kicking through some dry leaves and thinking about that, I heard a voice call out, "Becky!" I turned around. There was Megan, racing to catch up with me, panting and out of breath. I stopped and waited for her.

"Hi," I said.

"Hi," she gasped, bending over like she had a cramp from running.

While she was still doubled over, I said to the back of her curly red head, "Hey, actually, this is a little weird, but would you mind calling me Rebecca? Nobody ever called me Becky at home. That was kind of an accident the first day."

"Sure," she puffed, still bent over and breathing hard. She stood back up, and her hair frothed around her face.

"What's up?" I asked.

She giggled. "*You* are, you goof! Aren't you? How did it feel to say that stuff to Hannah?"

I blushed.

"I just wanted to tell you," she added, "that a lot of people were glad to see that happen. Everyone's talking about it. She's had that coming for a long time."

"Yeah," I said. "I didn't exactly plan it that way, but I guess she deserved it. She's so mean." I shook my head.

"She is," said Megan slowly. "But the thing you should know, the sad part, is that she wasn't always like that. She wasn't always so bad."

"She wasn't?" I was surprised.

"She's been my neighbor since preschool," said Megan, "and our moms are friends, so we've always been friends too. Then in fifth grade her dad moved away. He, like, *left* them."

"Oh," I said.

"Yeah," said Megan. "He works in New York now and travels a lot. He goes to Europe on business and sends her fancy presents, like that dumb jacket, but she never sees him. Ever since that all happened, she's been . . . different."

"I didn't know . . . ," I said.

Megan shrugged. "No reason you should. She never talks about him, except to brag about the stuff he buys her. I didn't mean to make you feel bad. Hannah is awful and she needed someone to tell her the truth. She had it coming. But I thought you should know that deep down she's a person still. Or I *think* she is, anyway."

"Wow," I said. "Wow."

I probably could have asked Megan over that day to hang out. We might have become real friends. But things at home were so weird. Plus, I had something I didn't want to put off any longer, something I needed to do. So we chatted for a few more minutes, about smaller things, and then I told her I had to get home. We said goodbye and went our separate ways.

I ran straight home to Gran's house, as fast as I could, with my locket knocking against my chest.

CHAPTER 17

The cab, when it pulled up in front of the coffee shop, was the wrong color. It was white, not yellow like cabs are supposed to be. That bothered me for some reason, but I got in anyway, with my backpack over one shoulder and a full black trash bag in my arms. It was awkward, climbing in.

I wished I could have said something to Gran and Lew at the house before I left. I'd have liked to have given them each a hug. Instead I'd snuck in and out as fast as I could, because I didn't want anyone to ask about the trash bag. In it were all the stolen goods. The TV and the iPod and the dead phone and the clothes and even the diamond. Everything except the things I'd given to Lew. And the spoon. That was in my backpack. Mom's charger I left in her room, on the floor, in hopes she'd assume she'd dropped it there.

"Where to?" asked the cabbie, turning his head to look back at me. He had an accent, but I could understand him easily enough. The music that played softly reminded me of my dad's favorite Indian restaurant. It made me feel hungry. Or maybe I was just nervous.

"I need to go to Clarkston," I said, dumping my backpack and the garbage bag beside me on the seat. "Will that be a lot of money?" The car smelled like smoke, even though there was a NO SMOKING sign on the window. "Clarkston, Georgia?" I wanted to make sure I had enough money.

The cabbie laughed. "Everything is far in Atlanta, but nothing is too far if you've got the correct amount of money. Maybe ten or fifteen minutes, depending. May I ask what is the exact address, please?" He was a very polite cabbie.

I opened the hand that held my tiny scrap of paper and read the address to him, even though I pretty much had it memorized.

"We will be there in no time." He nodded. "But first I must ask: Do your parents know where you are? It's unusual to pick up a fare so young in front of a coffee shop." He eyed my bag curiously. "You are not running away or anything?" He looked concerned.

"No," I said with a laugh, hoping I sounded normal. "My mom and dad know I'm here. They told me to call a cab. We're staying with my grandmother, a few streets over, on Woodland." I wasn't sure if I should be telling him where Gran lived, but he didn't seem creepy or anything.

The cabbie still didn't start the car. He sat there and looked at me. "May I ask—how old are you?"

"I'm thirteen," I said without blinking. I thought thirteen sounded a lot older than twelve. "I'm going to see my mom at her friend's house. My dad said to call a cab. He was busy." I was talking too much and I knew it. *Less is more.*

The cabbie squinted one eye at me for a minute. But at last he turned around and started the car.

I stared at the back of his head and said, "Hey, is there a Goodwill or anything on the way there? A Salvation Army? I need to drop this bag off if I can. Just some old stuff."

The cabbie looked back over his shoulder and eyed my bag again. "Yes," he said with a short nod. "There are several of them, actually. We can stop, no problem." Then he began to whistle along with the music.

He was a nice-enough-looking guy, baldish and smiley, with thick glasses and dark skin. His top half was a skinny person's top, and his bottom half, I couldn't help noticing when I leaned over the seat to talk to him, was a fat person's bottom. I wondered if maybe that just happened to people who sat down all day every day.

I watched the meter as the car began to move down the street, cruising slowly over the speed bumps. For a while we were driving on familiar roads, the same little streets

I'd been walking along with Lew for the last month. Then we turned onto a bigger road and cruised along past vacant buildings and construction projects before pulling into a cracked parking lot with a big red metal box in it that read DONATIONS, a kind of oversized mailbox.

It wasn't quite what I'd envisioned. I guess maybe I'd been hoping some nice old lady would "ooh" and "aah" over my wonderful gifts to the poor, make me feel generous and helpful, but the big metal box was what I had instead, so I opened it up. The door made a clanging, creaking sound as it opened. I pushed the huge bag into the yawning mouth of the box and let the door fall shut with a bang. I opened the door one more time and peered in. It was empty.

Good. All my ill-gotten goods were gone. I could never get them back, and I felt immediately relieved. I guess sometimes when you can't exactly fix a problem, you can at least discard it. I'd never thought about that before.

I climbed back into the cab. "Okay," I said. "Now Clarkston?"

"Onward to Clarkston," said the cabbie, and the car began to move again.

We passed empty strip malls, huge vacant lots, and gray apartment buildings. We passed a bunch of people standing around. This was not a pretty neighborhood.

At last I relaxed and sat back against an ancient leather

cushion that was held together with silver duct tape. I thought about what I was doing, where I was going. Now that I was headed in what I supposed was the right direction, I realized exactly what I'd done. I was in a cab, alone, at the age of twelve, heading to a complete stranger's house, in a part of town I'd never been to, in a city I didn't really know. I wasn't sure who I'd find when I got where I was going, or what, really, I'd say to them. But I had to admit that it was an adventure. I was certainly *doing* something.

I stared out the window at the world rushing past me. Trees and trees and so much green for such a big city, but all of it covered in litter and growing up through cracked cement. Everything I saw seemed to be either a blown-out old building, surrounded by barbed-wire fences and parking lots, or a lush green forest. What a weird place Atlanta was.

We shot along that wide road, and I found myself thinking about how I'd never read a book or seen a movie where a kid took off on an adventure all alone. Wasn't there always a friend or a sister or something? A helpful grown-up or at least a smart dog? I didn't even have a dog.

I wished someone else were with me. If all this had happened at home, I guess Mary Kate would have come too, maybe. Then again, all this wouldn't have happened at home.

If I'd waited a few weeks, maybe Megan and I would

really have become friends, and she would have come with me. Or maybe she wouldn't have. It was hard to tell.

I missed Lew.

The cab made a few turns, onto other wide streets. The neighborhood got prettier and fancier, with shops and things, but then, suddenly, we were driving alongside a railroad track, and it looked like we were in the country. There were little wooden houses and a few funny-looking junky antique stores. There was an old-fashioned gas station that looked abandoned. Were we still in Atlanta?

Then we were on a side street, and just as we were turning into the driveway of an old house, three hungry-looking stray dogs ran past us. The cab came to a stop. The meter said I owed the cabbie twelve dollars. I gave him a twenty. "Keep the change," I said.

He looked surprised.

"My dad used to drive a cab," I explained. It made me feel proud to say that, which was funny, since Mom had always seemed embarrassed of the fact.

"Used to?"

"He wrecked it," I said, realizing the cabbie now knew more about my dad than anyone else I'd met in Atlanta.

"That's too bad," he said.

"Yeah, it is," I said. For some reason I was having trouble getting out of the cab.

The cabbie looked at me and smiled kindly. "You want for me to wait here until you get inside?"

"Um, no, that's okay," I said, opening the door. "I might have to wait for them awhile or something. It'll be fine. Don't worry."

The cabbie shrugged. "If you say so."

I got out of the car and took a deep breath. I slammed the door behind me. I watched the car pull away. There was no going back.

I faced the house, a dingy brick box with dark orange trim. I held my breath as I walked up the concrete steps. At the top, I found a porch that was covered—*completely* covered—in plants.

Dead ones.

I was alone, all alone. I'd been feeling alone for weeks, but I hadn't really *been* alone, had I? Not until now, not really. I'd had Gran and Mom—even when I didn't want her—and Lew at least nearby. Now . . . they were all very far away.

What was I supposed to say? Did I just knock on the door and hand over the spoon? Then what? Turn around and go home? How? I hadn't thought about that. Maybe I should have asked the cabbie to stick around after all.

CHAPTER 18

I stood there, looking at the dead plants and feeling like I'd made a terrible mistake. There were cobwebs in the door frame. The rocking chair in front of me was covered in old newspapers and circulars from the grocery store. Cracked planters were stacked on top of one another at my feet. The place looked haunted. That was silly to even think; I knew that. It was just a dirty house, but it was very dirty.

Probably nobody was home.

I wiped away a few cobwebs and rang the doorbell. It made a buzzing sound, like a bee trapped in a jar. Nobody came to the door. I stared at the dead plants. I looked back over my shoulder, at the overgrown yard. I buzzed the bell again.

After a minute, I heard some noises inside: a groan, and then what sounded like someone moving something heavy, a box or a piece of furniture maybe. Next something fell. After that, silence.

Whatever I'd expected, it wasn't this. I really didn't know what to do. Should I ring the bell one more time? Should I wait? Should I run next door and see if I could find a neighbor? That falling sound had me worried. What if something was wrong inside?

I wanted to walk away from that house, but now I really couldn't. I decided to look for a neighbor in one of the other dingy brick boxes on the street, to see if maybe they could help.

Just as I was turning to walk down the steps, a key turned in the lock with a scraping sound, and the door opened about four inches. A tiny face peered out at me, a woman's face.

"Hello?" said the woman. "Hello?" She squinted. She seemed okay, pretty much, not healthy, exactly, but okay. At least she didn't look like *she* was the thing that had fallen.

Her face was pinched and lined. It looked like it had been dusted with flour. Her chin was pointy, her lips were smeared unevenly with orange lipstick, and there was a tiny white bun on the very top of her head. She was so small I was able to look down at the top of the bun. She reminded me of a bird.

"Hey," I said, turning back around to face her fully. Then I corrected myself. "I mean, hello, ma'am."

I guess because she was so old, I found myself suddenly talking like someone in an old-fashioned book. "Hey" felt like a bad word, too slangy. I bent down so that I was the same height as the woman. I had to resist a funny urge to curtsy.

When the old lady saw me, she opened the door a bit farther and smiled. Her eyebrows went up into her little forehead, and I noticed they were painted on. She was wearing a shapeless blue flowered dress and a pair of scruffy white slippers. She *was* really old.

"Why, hello," she said, and her voice took me by surprise. It stood out, like the orange lipstick. Her voice wasn't tiny. It was clear and sharp. Her voice sounded as strong as her body looked weak. Her eyes were bright in her white face, light blue and rimmed with a little bit of pink. They looked watery, but wide awake.

I decided I liked her.

"I rarely use this door," she said. "So I had to move a few things around to get to you, I'm afraid. That's why it took me so long. Can I help you?"

I hoped so, but I didn't have any idea how to begin. "I . . . um . . . I'm sorry to bother you. If now isn't a good time I can . . ." I didn't know what I *could* do. It wasn't as though I was going to come back later. I wasn't even sure how I planned to get home, but it seemed like the thing to say. "I mean, if you're busy—"

"Oh, heavens, no," said the old lady with a chuckle.

"I haven't been busy in decades. Not since my grandson grew up and moved to California. I'm pleased with the distraction. Can I help you?"

"Actually, I . . . um . . . I . . ." I knew I sounded like an idiot, stammering like that, but I really had no idea how to start. How did I tell her I'd come to bring her back an old, tarnished spoon that she probably didn't even remember?

"Don't be frightened, dear," she said with a laugh. "I won't bite you." Her laugh sounded old-fashioned too. Southern, but also proper, like something from an old movie my dad would fall asleep watching. She stretched back her head when she laughed. "Are you selling cookies or something like that? For school?"

I took a deep breath. "No. I'm not selling anything. I just . . . have something I want to show you, if . . . well, if you're . . . Are you Adda?"

She laughed again. "Usually I'm called *Miss* Adda by people your age, but, yes, that's me. I think you've got the right house."

I nodded. "And so . . . Harlan is—"

Miss Adda's face fell. "Oh. He's dead, dear. Harlan is dead." Her orange mouth frowned and mostly disappeared.

"I'm sorry. I didn't mean to . . . I just—"

"Don't apologize. It's fine," said Miss Adda, though she still looked sad. "I mean, it *isn't* fine. But it's been years and years, and I'm mostly used to it now."

"I'm still sorry," I offered.

"That's kind," she said. "Me too."

I didn't know what else to add to that. My backpack was slipping, so I hefted it farther onto my shoulder.

"Well," said Miss Adda. "Now that I'm who you want me to be, would you maybe like to come in and tell me who *you* are? I don't often have guests, so it's a bit of a mess in here." She glanced behind herself and looked nervous. "But I'm pleased to have company, and I can make a pot of tea."

"I'm not sure," I said. "I don't mean to be a bother—"

"You're not, dear, but I just don't want to stand up forever like this on the porch. It's chilly out here, and my arthritis—"

"Oh, of course," I said. I hadn't thought about her standing there in the cold in that thin dress.

I knew I wasn't supposed to go anywhere with strangers, but after all, *I* was the one who'd come knocking. I'd disturbed her, so I should go inside and let her sit down. It was only polite.

But when I stepped inside after Miss Adda, I felt less sure about my decision. In fact, I wanted to run back out. I found myself staring down a dark hallway full of junk. This hallway made Gran's attic look like a showroom at a department store. Along each wall was a long bookshelf, bursting with a strange assortment of books, antiques, and garbage. China figurines and balls of rubber bands, dishes of hard candy and stacks of old newspapers. Broken toys. Everything on the bookshelves in the dim hall looked about to spill over. The bookshelves themselves appeared to be leaning, as if they might cave inward at any second.

The floor was even worse! It was covered in boxes and bags of old clothes, plastic trash cans full of coat hangers. Recycling bins full of everything *but* recycling. One box seemed to hold nothing but old records without their jackets, just black plastic disks stacked and crammed together. By my right foot was a bucket full of twisted and tangled beaded necklaces. By my left foot was an open garbage bag crammed with dingy white leather purses, as far as I could tell.

Finding a path through the mess was tricky, like walking down a stream on stepping-stones. I had to look for clear bits of carpet. Miss Adda was well ahead of me. She knew where to step. It must have been like this for years.

Halfway down the hall, I stepped over a birdcage lying on the ground. I thought maybe that explained the crash I'd heard, because as I made my way past it, I felt birdseed grinding into the rug under my feet. But that wasn't the bad part. The bad part was that inside the birdcage was a bird. A bird that looked like it had been dead for a long, long time.

Ahead of me, Miss Adda was stepping into a rectangle of light at the end of the hall, heading into another room.

I wondered what I'd find there.

CHAPTER 19

M iss Adda's kitchen didn't look like any kitchen I'd ever been in before, mostly because it was so green. There was a green tablecloth on the table, and in the center of it were several sets of green salt and pepper shakers arranged around a little vase with a green silk flower in it. The flower was dusty, but it was all *just so*. The walls were papered with a glossy pattern of forest branches. None of the chairs matched, except for the fact that they were painted green. At one end of the room was a glass door that led out to a little back porch, which appeared to house some actual living plants. I could see their tendrils curling against the glass. At the other end of the room was an open doorway, hung with a green curtain. It was weird how completely green the room was, but it was a nice-enough place. Clearly it was exactly how she wanted it to be. Nobody ended up with a kitchen like that by accident.

Despite the weird amount of green, looking around the kitchen made me feel better about Miss Adda's house. The counters were mostly clear and clean. There weren't gross food messes or anything. The trash wasn't overflowing. It didn't smell bad. Still, it was sad to imagine Miss Adda eating alone there. Washing a single cup. She'd said she didn't often have visitors, and I wondered how often she got to the store. I wondered if she was able to drive a car. I hadn't seen one out front.

Miss Adda was busy, filling a kettle at the rust-stained sink. She set it on the stove and reached for a tin of tea from a little shelf. "So, dear," she said, "where do you live?"

I sat down in one of the green chairs and thought about that. It took me a minute to say. "Well . . . Baltimore."

"Baltimore?" She turned around. "You're an extremely long way from home."

"Yeah, I know," I said with a sigh. Then I added, "But I'm staying with my gran right now—not far away from here."

"Oh, that's nice for your gran! Nice for everyone, I'm sure," Adda said, bobbing her tiny head up and down.

"I guess so," I said. "I *guess* it is."

Adda turned back around to the stove, where the kettle was starting to steam.

"I like your kitchen," I said, staring up at a green glass chandelier. "I like how everything is a different kind of green."

Miss Adda turned away from the stove and beamed at

me. "Oh! I'm *so* glad you noticed!" she said. "Green is my favorite color. It's so alive, so fresh, but not everybody sees all the different greens, you know—some people just see *green*. Doesn't that sound boring to you? Wouldn't you hate to be one of those people?"

I thought about that. I *was* glad to see all the greens, though it seemed a funny thing for her to say.

In a minute, Miss Adda set up a little tray with a sugar bowl and two cups and a fat little teapot. It was cute, something old ladies were supposed to do, though I'd never seen one actually do it. I didn't know many old ladies very well, besides Gran, and she wasn't *that* old.

Miss Adda carried the tray very carefully over to the table. It made a tinkling sound as she slid it in front of me. Her arms shook.

I looked down and noticed that there were sprays of fern all over the cups. They looked so delicate. When I reached out to touch one with a finger, the porcelain felt as thin as glass, fragile.

"Pretty," I said.

"Thank you. They are, aren't they? It's my wedding china. Kept it on the shelf for years and years, but I don't see any reason not to use it now. What on earth was I saving it for?" She turned back to the counter for a plate of cookies.

There were some very old-looking napkins the color of new grass on the tray too, edged in dark green lace.

They were stained, but ironed to a crease as sharp as a knife. I took one and put it in my lap.

"Milk, dear?" Miss Adda asked, standing by the sink.

I nodded.

Miss Adda reached for a box that said "nonfat dry milk." She shook the box right into the cream pitcher, then added water, stirring it quickly with a fork. I'd never seen powdered milk before. It reminded me of the formula Dad had sometimes given Lew when he was a baby and Mom had to work late.

Miss Adda brought the pitcher and the plate of cookies to the table and sat down slowly in the chair opposite me. She poured us each a cup of tea, adding the milk to both. The milk smelled funny and left bubbles on the surface of the tea. There were lumps. I don't know why that was so disgusting to me, but it was. I had to work hard at not wrinkling my nose. I was afraid of what would happen if I actually tasted it, so I just pretended to sip my tea and said, "Mmmmmm . . ." The cup warmed my hands.

Miss Adda clutched her tea. She sat on the very edge of her seat, which was a ladder-back chair painted a forest green.

"I can't tell you how nice it is to have a visitor for tea on a cold day," she said.

"Thank you for inviting me," I said, remembering my manners.

"Certainly." She nodded. "Although, when you rang, I almost didn't come to the door. I figured it was someone selling something, or the police wanting me to cut the grass, or maybe a nice lady wanting to tell me about Jesus. As if by the age of ninety-three I haven't decided what I think, or don't think, about our Lord. They always tell me there's still time left. What they don't say is that there isn't *much* time left."

I wasn't sure how to respond to that, but Miss Adda didn't seem upset. She was matter-of-fact about it. She looked me in the eye and said, "There isn't, you know— much time—but that's okay."

I shifted in my chair and picked up my cup. "We don't have to talk about—"

"Why not?" Miss Adda asked. She stared up at me. "Why *shouldn't* we?"

I stared back uncomfortably. "I don't know," I said.

"Why do people *never* want to talk to old folks about dying?" asked Miss Adda. "Heaven knows we think about it an awful lot. Why, we know more about death than anyone!"

She paused and sat there, like she was waiting for me to actually answer her. She just sat there, looking at me, gripping her teacup, waiting.

"I guess . . . ," I said at last. "I guess because it scares us. Death, I mean. And getting old. I guess we're trying not to think about it. And you remind us of it?" This felt like a terrible thing to say, but it was what came out.

"Hmm. That's probably true," said Miss Adda. She poured herself some more tea.

I pretended to sip mine again.

Miss Adda's orange mouth curved gently into a smile. "Is your tea too strong? You don't have to drink it, you know."

"Um, just a little," I said with relief. I set my cup down.

"I'm sorry to sound like a batty old bird," said Miss Adda. "But I spend all day alone with the radio and whatever is out my window, and none of it talks back very often. So I forget how to be polite, I suppose. I forget my manners, after all those years thinking about them. Funny, they don't seem so important now." Miss Adda stared off, out toward the glass door. She seemed lost in her thoughts, and I didn't interrupt her. Then she turned back to stare at me and said suddenly, "But this isn't what you came here for. What *did* you come here for? You said you have something to show me?"

"Oh yes!" I said. I couldn't believe I'd gotten distracted for this long. "I do! Let me get it."

As I leaned down to reach into my backpack, I felt nervous, tingly, almost scared. Then, rooting around in my bag, I couldn't find the spoon!

"Hang on," I said. "I'm sure it's here. I know I brought it." I lifted the bag to my knees to paw around inside it, but I still couldn't find the spoon. Was it possible I'd lost it, after all this trouble? I stood up and walked over to the counter, where I set down the bag under the overhead light and practically stuck my whole head inside it.

At last I saw a silver gleam. There it was! Tucked away beneath a fold of fabric, buried under my sweater. I pulled it out, breathed on it, and shined it against my shirt.

I whirled around and held the spoon out to Adda. "Found it! Here it is!" I called out, elated. "Look!"

Across the room, Miss Adda stood up. Her eyes widened as they settled on the spoon. Her mouth opened. Her chin went down.

"Oh," she said. She looked stunned. "Oh!" She gasped as she fell against the table, caught herself, but then pushed herself back up.

The table wobbled. The tray of tea things shook too, then slid and tipped onto the floor. All the dishes crashed against the tile and shattered. The thin, lumpy milk and tea ran together and made a puddle all over the floor. Sugar scattered.

I looked over at the floor below Miss Adda's feet. "Oh no. I'm sorry!" I said. I reached for a dishcloth that hung over the faucet beside me. Then I froze.

Miss Adda had such a strange look on her face. She didn't even seem to notice that she was standing in a puddle of milky tea. She just stood there, her eyes fixed like laser beams on the spoon in my outstretched hand.

At last she mouthed, "It . . . can't . . . be."

She moved toward me quickly, pushing through shards of china in her soft slippers, and grabbed the spoon, as if she were in a trance.

"Where? How? Where . . . ," she babbled, wrapping her fingers around the spoon.

I let go of the spoon, and she pulled it close to her face to read the inscription out loud. "'To Adda. From Harlan. With love,'" she whispered softly. Then she clutched it to her chest. "It really is the spoon," she said. "*Our* spoon. How did you—"

"I *knew* it was yours!" I shouted happily.

Miss Adda's face shifted. It was like watching weather change. The trance faded. Her orange mouth drew into a tiny smudge, the lips pinched and tight. Her eyes slitted. Her painted brows lowered, and her shoulders hunched. She shook the spoon in the air, in front of my face.

"*How* did you get this?" she demanded. *"How?"*

"I . . . I bought it . . . ," I said, confused. "In a junk store, for my mom."

"Liar," she spat, jabbing the spoon in my direction. I took a step back.

She said it again: *"Liar!"* Like she was stabbing me with both the spoon and the word. "Thief!"

My heart began to race. How could she possibly know that? What was going on?

"I don't know how you did this," Miss Adda said in a strange hissing voice. "I don't know why you did this! *Why* did you do this thing?" She jabbed again, pushing at the air in front of her with the spoon.

"I don't know! I didn't mean to—" I cried, taking another step back.

The weather shifted again. Like a sudden storm, Miss Adda's tiny face crumpled and she began to weep, standing there in the middle of that green room. She cried deep, deep sobs, clutching the spoon to her chest. Her whole body shook.

I didn't know what to do. I didn't know what I had done. What had happened to her? How could I help? I felt like I should comfort her, but I was scared to touch her.

"I was only trying to—" I started, reaching out a hand.

Miss Adda jerked her head up, and her eyes opened wide. "Cruel!" she shouted. "You horrid girl. You . . . grave robber!" Then she reached up and raged at me with her bony little arms, the way Lew does when he's having a temper tantrum. She was almost like a baby, helpless, waving her arms in the air.

Even so, I was scared. Her arms scared me suddenly, those twiggy, pale, helpless arms. I didn't want them to touch me and I panicked. I leaned away from those spotted, tiny hands, stretching back, back, back—and fell.

The green curtain brushed lightly against my back, and then cold air whipped past me, enclosed me, as I felt myself falling and tumbling, clattering down a flight of stairs my feet couldn't seem to find. My knees banged against a step and then another as the side of my face slapped into a wall. I managed to twist myself, grabbing wildly, and I caught hold of a splintery railing, stopping myself from falling any farther. Then I knelt like that. Just like that, clutching the railing, halfway down the stairs. I just needed to hold on to something. I could feel my nose bleeding. I could taste blood. My arms were scraped. I felt like one big bruise. What had just happened?

I looked above me, squinting up the stairs. I saw Miss Adda's thin body silhouetted in a rectangle of light, holding aside the curtain. Her voice sounded witchlike as she called down at me, "You can just wait *there*!"

A door slammed shut and I was lost in total darkness. It was like something from one of the mystery novels I'd been reading.

All I could think was, *Grave robber?*

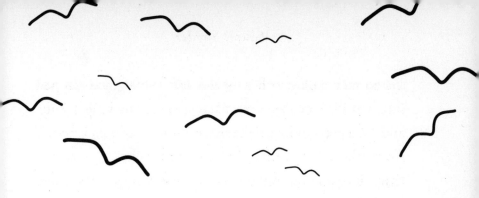

Chapter 20

I sat there on the step and felt at my legs and arms. I clenched and unclenched my hands. Nothing was broken. Nothing hurt badly enough to be serious. So I sat there in the pitch black, tilting my head and pinching my nose and trying to figure out what had just happened.

"Grave robber?" I whispered. *That* didn't make any sense at all. Maybe Miss Adda was just plain bonkers. Maybe I'd stumbled into the home of a truly sick person. Maybe she had Alzheimer's. Maybe she had multiple personalities or something scary like that. She had changed her mood so suddenly! I thought about the dead bird and what she'd said about "seeing all the greens." She wasn't okay. I could see that now.

But crazy or not, even though I was banged up pretty badly and I wanted out of that basement, I still felt sorry for her. Poor old lady. Waving her arms and screeching, she seemed so lost and wild and sad. I thought about her shuffling through the broken teacups, the dusty silk flower in the vase, the powdered milk.

Still, I had to get out!

I pushed myself to standing and inched my way back up the stairs. I kept one hand on the rough wooden railing and the other hand flat against the cement wall beside me, trying to find a light switch. Instead I found that the wall beside the staircase was hung with heavy metal tools. I felt a big wrench and a shovel. I knocked something small, like a screwdriver, loose and listened to it fall down the steps in a series of clunks and thunks. I'd been lucky in my fall. I could have easily smashed my head into a rusty saw.

Reaching the top, I felt the kitchen door against my shoulder. I grabbed for where the doorknob should have been, but there wasn't a doorknob to grab on to, just a wedge of wood. I pushed against the door with all my strength and it shook, but the latch didn't give way. It was dead bolted or something. I was trapped.

I ran my hands along the wall all around the door, thinking there had to be a light switch somewhere, but when at last I found one, it clicked uselessly. I guess Miss Adda wasn't tall enough to change the lightbulb. There were an awful lot of things someone like Miss Adda probably couldn't do.

It had been horrible, watching her shift from a nice old lady into a crazy person. She hadn't seemed violent, but she was so old. Maybe the shock of seeing that spoon had just pushed her over the edge. I didn't think she'd meant to hurt me or trap me in the dark. She was like a cat or something, lashing out with her little claws.

Finally I did the only thing I could think of—I knocked at the door, as though it were a normal door, the front door of a house, as though I were starting over, paying Miss Adda a regular visit.

"Miss Adda?" I called out. "Hello? Miss Adda?"

It felt bizarre to knock from inside that dark cellar.

When she didn't respond, I put my ear to the crack of the door and pushed gently with my shoulder. The door didn't budge.

On the other side, Miss Adda was sobbing quietly. She sounded like some kind of old, broken machine. Her cries were tiny jerking sounds, little tugs and chokes.

"Miss Adda?"

"What do you want now?" she called out.

I thought that was pretty obvious. I wanted out. But I didn't say that. Instead I said, "I want to apologize. I'm sorry, Miss Adda. I really am. . . ."

She just kept crying.

I tried again. "Please? Let me out?"

This time the crying stopped. "You have to wait," she said. "For the police."

Had she really called the police? "But . . . I'm scared down here," I said. "It's dark."

"So? What *isn't?*" asked Miss Adda.

"Please," I said. "Let me out. You don't need to call the police. I didn't mean to steal anything," I said. "It was an accident."

"How can *that* be?" cried Miss Adda with a sad little laugh. "How do you steal something by accident?" Miss Adda blew her nose, then continued. "How do you *accidentally* rob a casket?"

It was my turn to be bewildered. "Casket?"

"I buried that spoon with him myself," she said. "Slid it into his pocket just before they closed him up, just before I kissed him goodbye." She started to cry again, shuddering through the words. "Before they slid him into that cold, cold ground forever."

Then I understood, and shivered. I remembered the cold, thin metal of that spoon the first time I held it. I remembered taking it out of the bread box and pressing it against my cheek. I could almost feel it between my fingers now, and I wanted to throw up in the darkness, knowing where the spoon had come from: a dark, cold place in the earth.

Miss Adda kept talking. "It was the finest thing he ever gave me, for our twenty-fifth wedding anniversary. You might just think it's a spoon, but it isn't. It's very rare. Valuable. A special spoon. It was his mother's to begin with, but he had it engraved for me. So then I gave it back to him, when he left me. To keep. Until I could join him."

"Oh," I said.

"And you took it from him, just like that! So now I'm going to call the police on you, like I would for any thief!" I heard her pick up a phone, heard the faint sound of a bell as she lifted the old-fashioned receiver. I wondered what on earth the police would do when they came. Would they believe her? And even if they didn't, how would I explain any of this to my mom when I came home in a squad car?

"Please, just let me out," I said. "I'll try to explain."

"No!" said Miss Adda. "You can wait for them to come and take you away—you can wait down there in the dark. Alone. Like poor Harlan. Besides, how can you possibly explain?"

I shivered. I couldn't tell if she'd hung up the phone.

"I . . . didn't mean to," I said quietly. "It's so complicated. I *did* steal it, I guess, but I didn't know I was doing it. I made a mistake. I was wrong. I was selfish, and I'm sorry. But I wasn't *trying* to take your spoon."

I *was* sorry. I shouldn't have taken the spoon. I shouldn't have taken anything. I regretted it all now. The magic only made everything worse. Wishes were curses. I took a deep breath. Miss Adda didn't understand, and she never would unless . . . Should I tell her everything? The truth was all I had left, and maybe, maybe she'd let me out if she understood what had really happened. Was there any chance she was crazy enough to believe me?

"Would you believe me," I asked, "if I told you it was magic?"

She didn't answer me at first. So I knocked at the door again and said, "Miss Adda? Did you hear what I said?"

"I . . . I might," she said at last. "I *might* believe you."

So I told her. I told her everything. It all came tumbling out, the whole mess of a story. I told her about the fight and the move, about hiding in the attic and finding the bread box, about the seagulls that first night, and everything after . . .

It took a minute before Miss Adda said, "I don't . . . know. I don't know if I can believe that." She took a deep, shuddery breath, the kind of breath that means you're done crying. "But I'd like to."

I heard her return the phone to its cradle. Had she been holding it the whole time?

"It's true," I said. "I don't understand it myself, but it's all true."

"I want to believe you. I do," said Miss Adda. "Because maybe if I can believe you, if I can believe in magic, the way I believe in other things—trees, or rocks, or pancakes, or my tired body, or anything else I *know* is real— maybe if I can believe in magic, I can believe all the other things I see. Does that sound crazy?"

It *did* sound crazy. Totally nuts. But I could tell she was standing just on the other side of the door now, inches away from me. I could hear her breathing between sentences. I thought she might still open the door.

"No, it doesn't sound crazy to me," I said through the crack. I tried to make my voice sound as kind as I could. "It doesn't sound crazy at all."

Miss Adda kept talking. "Have you ever lost someone you loved?" she asked me.

"I have," I said. For a moment I could smell my father in the dark stairwell, the smoke on his shirt, though it was probably just the lingering smoke from the cab on my own clothes. "I have." I knew it wasn't what Miss Adda meant, but it felt true.

"I'm so alone," said Miss Adda. "And it's so hard. Waking up each day. Knowing that I'll never see him again in this world. That all the things I never said to him are inside me, waiting, and they will just have to live there forever, unsaid. Thinking of all the things we can never do again together. The cup of coffee I'll never bring him. The umbrella he'll never hold over my head in the rain."

"I'm sorry," I said. I didn't know what else to say.

"I am too," came the sad voice from the other side of the door. "I am too."

Then Miss Adda got lost in her memories, I guess, the coffee and the rain, because she started to cry again. Her weeping got fainter and fainter. I could tell she was walking away. I heard her shuffling again in the shards of china.

"Miss Adda?" I called out, panicked. "Hello? Are you still there?"

It was too late. She didn't answer me this time. Maybe because she didn't hear me, or maybe because she was drowning in the past, lost in her memories.

I stood there in the dark at the top of the stairs, waiting. Then I realized there was nothing to wait for, and I started to yell. "HELLLLLLLLLP!" I called out as loud as I could. "HELLLLLLLLLLLLP! Please, let me out!" But as loud as I was, nobody came.

Finally my voice got hoarse and I gave up on Miss Adda. I made my way back down the stairs to where I'd felt the wrench hanging on the wall and I took it down. Then I went back to the door and began to hit at the old wood near the dead bolt, right at the crack where the door met the frame. At first I was tapping more than pounding. The wrench was so heavy I was almost afraid I might throw my weight too far back and fall down the stairs again. But the more I tapped, the more confident I got, until I was really banging at that door. I could feel splinters and flakes of paint chipping. I could feel the door heaving. Small bits of wood began to fall to the ground. At some point I realized that I *would* eventually break through, unless Miss Adda got sick of hearing me bang and let me out.

I thought about everything that had happened. *BANG!* About the bread box and the spoon. *BANG!* About my dad. *BANG!* About my mom. I thought about what I'd say to

Mom and to Dad, about the things I wasn't mad about anymore and the things I still was.

I started to get hungry, so then I thought about how I wanted a hamburger. *BANG!* It must be dinnertime by now. *BANG!* I thought about making my hamburger a cheeseburger.

I wondered how long I'd been gone. I wondered what my mom was doing. *BANG!* Maybe she was still mad enough that she didn't care. *BANG! BANG!*

I was banging so hard I didn't hear what was happening on the other side of the door. Suddenly the door flew open.

Light flooded into my eyes, and I squinted in the bright glare, my wrench raised. I almost pounded into the chest of a very tall man in a police uniform. He stared down at me in surprise as I dropped my wrench. We studied each other in silence as the tool thumped down the basement steps behind me.

"Who are *you?*" the policeman asked. His teeth were very white in his dark face, even in the shadow of the basement stairwell, and his voice was gentle.

Behind him, another officer, a woman with a blond ponytail, was struggling to walk Miss Adda away. Miss Adda was crying.

I looked back up at the cop in front of me, confused.

"Who are you?" he asked again.

Still I didn't answer.

"You okay?" he asked kindly.

Then I started to cry. I couldn't help it. I didn't even try to help it, not this time. I just fell apart. He was so big and strong-looking. I was, well, a kid who'd fallen down half a flight of stairs and then been locked in a strange basement. I lost it.

The policeman seemed to take everything in—my bloody nose, my messy hair, my tears—and he leaned forward and scooped me up, as easily as if I were Lew, and carried me out of that awful house in his big arms, through the green kitchen and the gross hallway, past Miss Adda arguing with the other officer on the front steps. I remember his badge scratching my arm. I closed my eyes and let myself be carried.

The policeman sct mc down on the sidewalk, next to his squad car, a little ways from the house. The sunlight was almost gone. It was cold outside, and I'd left my jacket in the kitchen, but it felt good, all that cold, fresh air. I sucked it in and looked around. The officer who'd carried me out was hunting around in the car for something, so I just waited.

Behind me, I could hear the policewoman wrestling Miss Adda away, through the yard and down the street. I didn't want to see Miss Adda, so I didn't turn around until she really started yelling. Then I looked down the block and saw the policewoman was trying to get her into another squad car.

Everything was happening very fast, too fast. I watched Miss Adda, in her blue dress and soggy slippers, slap at the officer. She looked different outside her house. She looked worse somehow, more crazy. Her bun had come loose, and her hair looked like the fake spiderwebs people decorate with on Halloween.

It was my fault, this mess, whatever was happening to Miss Adda. None of this would be happening if I hadn't come here and scared her. I noticed her skinny legs sticking out of the car door after the rest of her was pushed inside. I could hear her manic voice, from a distance, yelling, "No! No! *She's* the one. Take her. She took my spoon! With her magic! My spooooooooon!"

The other squad car drove off with Miss Adda, leaving behind a sad old slipper on the sidewalk. I didn't want to look at the slipper, so I turned to stare at the nice policeman who was climbing back out of his car. He was holding a gigantic blue sweater, which he handed to me.

"How did you know to come here?" I asked, wiping my nose with my arm before putting on the too-large sweater. "How did you find me?"

"Actually," he said, "we're not exactly sure what happened. Someone—I guess Mrs. Tompkins there—dialed nine-one-one from the house and then hung up. So we made a routine stop. When she came to the door, we heard you banging, and it all just seemed way too funny not to take a look. When we tried to come inside and she hit Officer Griggs in the face with a spoon, we decided she needed to go to the station for a while. We've talked with Mrs. Tompkins before, about other matters, but they were always little things—nothing like this has ever happened."

"She didn't mean to lock me down there," I explained. "She was in shock. I didn't want for this to happen. What will you do to her?"

"That's really for a doctor to decide now," said the officer. "But that lady needs some help, any way you look at it. She was saying some nutty things."

"Yeah," I said. I could imagine what she'd been saying.

Then it was like the policeman realized that he was talking to a kid. His tone changed and he asked me, "Now, what's *your* name, honey?"

"Rebecca," I said. "Rebecca Rose Shapiro."

"Well, Rebecca Rose Shapiro, I'm Officer Johnson. What say we get in the car, where it's warmer, and then see if we can't get you home to your parents. They'll need to help you decide what to do next. Whether you want to press charges or not."

"I don't," I said.

"Let's just get you home," he insisted.

I nodded and slid into the car, thinking, *Home. If only he could.*

Chapter 21

I expected Officer Johnson to have a clipboard or a computer. From TV shows I'd seen, I thought he'd want to take a statement. I figured he'd have to call someone on a CB or a radio or something. But none of that happened. In fact, he didn't do anything but put the key in the ignition and ask, "Now, where do you live?"

"Baltimore," I said right away. Then, because I didn't want him thinking I was some kind of runaway, I added quickly, "But I'm staying with my grandmother right now, on a street called Woodland, kind of over near the zoo. Do you know where that is?"

He turned back to look at me. "Are your parents staying there with you?" He looked a little concerned.

"Well, my parents—they aren't exactly together right now," I said. "We're staying—my mom and brother and me—with my grandmother while Mom . . . um . . .

figures things out. Just the last few weeks, I mean." I took a deep breath. "I guess they're . . . separated." As I said it, I realized I hadn't said that word to anyone before. I didn't think I'd even said it to myself.

Officer Johnson looked at me with sad eyes and said softly, "I'm sorry to hear that, Rebecca."

"It's okay," I said, even though it really wasn't.

"Maybe we should try calling your mom before we head over there. Just in case."

I nodded. In case of *what*? I wasn't sure. But I said "Okay," and told him Mom's cell phone number.

I watched him dial, but almost immediately, he hung up. "It went straight to voice mail," he said. "How about we call your grandmother?"

"What about my dad?" I asked. "Can't we call him? He's my *dad*."

"Sure," said Officer Johnson. "We can call him if you want, but right now our main concern is just getting you home, and you said he's in Baltimore, right? So maybe let's try your grandmother first."

"Yeah," I said. "But Gran's number is unlisted."

"And you don't know it?"

"I can't remember," I said, looking at my lap. "I had it in my phone but I . . . lost the phone." This all sounded so . . . neglected. I knew that, but it was just that things were weird right now. This would never have happened at home. "Can't you just drive me to her house?"

"I'd really like to make sure you've got someone waiting for you first," he said. "Under the circumstances."

"Circumstances? What do you mean?"

"Well . . ." He looked a little uncomfortable. "Just . . . we like to talk to a grown-up before we go dropping kids off, but I guess we can try your dad next if you want to."

Dad didn't answer either. Officer Johnson's glances were getting more and more worried, and I was feeling more and more pathetic.

"Please," I begged. "Can't you just take me home? I just want this to be over. Please?"

"I guess that's the next step," he said. "If you really think they're there. If they're not, we'll have to figure something else out."

"They'll be there," I said, nodding furiously. "Even if Mom's working, Gran never goes anywhere at night. She goes to bed early, and so does my brother, Lew." It was past dinnertime. Surely they'd be home. "They're just not good with phones."

Officer Johnson drove me back home, along the same wide roads the cabdriver had taken, past the same vacant lots and industrial buildings, which looked even more deserted in the darkness. A few times he turned on his siren briefly so he could run a red light, and we were there in no time. When we turned onto Gran's cozy street and I saw the porch light shining yellow from a block away, relief washed over me.

But nobody was there. Inside, the house was dark and empty. We knocked and knocked, but nobody came to the door, so we walked slowly back to the sidewalk and got into the car.

"Maybe they're looking for me at the police station?" I said hopefully.

"Maybe," he said, reaching for his phone.

I sat there in the squad car, staring at the house, while Officer Johnson called the department to see if my mom had reported me missing. That took a while because someone there had to check the computer system or something. As the moments ticked by, I got increasingly nervous. I wished and wished for them to come home. I willed them to pull up with takeout. I crossed my fingers and wondered what had happened. If they weren't just picking up a pizza or something, where could they be?

Then Officer Johnson hung back up and said apologetically, "Nope, I'm so sorry, but nobody's reported you missing. I don't think I have any choice but to take you over to DFCS for the night. Just for the night."

"DFCS?"

"Department of Family and Children Services. My shift is ending, and I've got to take you somewhere, Rebecca." He really looked like he felt terrible saying that, which made me more worried than anything else. "You'll be better off there than at the station."

Department of Family and Children Services? That was where you went when you didn't *have* parents. Or when you had horrible parents. Or when your horrible parents went to jail. Kids like me didn't go to DFCS. *I* wasn't supposed to go to DFCS!

"Please, just a minute longer?" I begged as he put the key into the ignition. "I'm sure they'll be here soon. They're probably out looking around the neighborhood for me. Or can I just go knock again, please? One last time? Maybe they were all up in the attic and didn't hear you or something. . . ."

He nodded, but it was in an apologetic way. "Here," he said, taking out a notepad and scribbling something on it. "While you're at it, you can leave this on the door for them in case they come back." He tore off the piece of paper and handed it to me as I opened my door.

Walking up the steps, I started to get very, very scared. Where *was* everyone? Had something awful happened to Lew? Why wasn't my mother's phone on when I was missing? Didn't she even care that I was gone?

I stood there, ringing the bell, which glowed like a little light. I peered through the glass door. For the first time since I could remember, I really wanted my mom. I wanted Gran too. I wanted to see Lew's little face peek around the corner. But most of all, I needed my mother.

I left the note on the door.

Five minutes later, we were driving in silence, and

ten minutes after that, Officer Johnson was stopping at a Wendy's for hamburgers. We ate our burgers without saying much. After a bit, Officer Johnson wiped his mouth with a napkin and said, "I've been wondering, why did you go to Mrs. Tompkins's house in the first place, Rebecca?"

Sitting there in the overheated restaurant, a version of the story tumbled out of me. I told him that I'd found a spoon with an inscription, and I'd wanted to return it to Miss Adda. I told him that I'd turned up on Miss Adda's doorstep, and she'd invited me in for tea, but when I'd shown her the spoon, she'd gotten upset and started crying and yelling because of her husband being dead and all, and because she thought—for *some* reason—I'd stolen the spoon.

I basically told him everything *except* the part about the bread box, and it was funny how the entire story held together without the magic, without the *how*. It was almost like the magic didn't really matter to the story at all. The last thing I said was "And when Miss Adda started to get all crazy, I kind of backed away from her, and when I did that, I fell down the stairs."

"*Fell?*"

"Yes," I said. "I fell. I really did." That wasn't a lie. I *had* fallen. "She did lock the door behind me," I admitted, "but I mean, she thought I had stolen from her, and she wanted to keep me there so that you could arrest me. She was confused, and mostly she was really, well, upset. I don't think she knew what she was doing."

Officer Johnson wadded up his hamburger wrapper and took a sip of his Coke. "You know, Rebecca," he said, "you're really not supposed to go into strangers' homes. Hasn't anyone ever told you that?"

"I know that," I said, "but she seemed so little."

"Rebecca. You're really not supposed to go *anywhere* with a stranger, even a *little* stranger. You got really lucky."

"I know," I said. "I *know*. I screwed up. You have no idea how bad I feel. Really. I'm sorry to trouble you, and my mom is going to kill me when she finds me, and I'm sorry for Miss Adda too." Then I looked up at him. "Where is she now?"

"She's on her way to being evaluated," he said. "To see if she should be living alone. And they'll try to track down her family, in case she needs someone to make decisions for her." Then he leaned over and gave me a pat on the back. "Don't worry. You're doing her a favor. Trust me. She needs some help no matter what. That *house*! It happens when people get old and they're all alone."

I thought about that. I remembered the dead bird in the cage, the burned-out bulbs, the powdered milk. For my own sake, I wanted Officer Johnson to be right. If he was right, I'd actually helped her, maybe. Instead of just making her life worse by trying to make myself feel better. I hoped that was true.

We left Wendy's and drove some more, and then we were pulling into a dark parking lot.

I didn't want to get out of the car. "Can't we try calling my mom?" I asked. "One more time?"

"I'm sorry, Rebecca," Officer Johnson said. "But time's up. I've been as nice as I can about this, and I'm sure you'll work it all out in the morning. I know you don't feel like you should be here, but for all intents and purposes, you're a lost kid right now. We can't locate your folks, and this is where we take lost kids when we can't find their folks." He looked tired.

I got out of the car and closed the door slowly behind me. I followed Officer Johnson across the parking lot, past a few cars and some shrubs. I didn't want to go in; I didn't belong here. I *had* a home. I did.

I stopped in front of the door. Officer Johnson put his hand on my back gently and said, "It'll be fine, really. I promise. Whatever happens." Then he opened the door and pushed me into the glaring light of an office. He motioned for me to sit down and then went to the desk. He said something I couldn't hear to the woman who was sitting behind it.

As she leaned forward to say something to him, looking up at me as she spoke, the door swung open again behind us, fast, with a jangle of bells.

And in walked . . . my dad!

CHAPTER 22

And after.
   After that.
   After Dad ran over and picked me up from the chair and swung me around and held me, I cried and cried.
   "*You're* here!" I said. "You're here. How are you here?"
   "I am," he said. "I just am. I'm sorry it took me so long. Your mom wasn't ready for me to be here. I'm still not sure she is. . . ."
   Then Mom ran in behind him, looking scared and frazzled, and I hugged her too. She hugged me back so hard I thought my ribs would break when she let me go.
   After that I went to stand with Dad, holding his hand, while Mom talked and talked and talked too much and too loudly to Officer Johnson. I could tell she was nervous because she didn't stop waving her hands in the air the whole time.

"We should have looked for her sooner," I heard her say. "I know that. I *know* how this looks, but really, we're good parents. Things have just been . . . complicated lately. I mean, that's no excuse. I should have been worried when Rebecca wasn't around when I got home from work, but she does that sometimes. Kids do, you know?" Mom took a deep breath.

Officer Johnson and the woman behind the desk looked like they were listening very carefully, and I hoped my mom wasn't saying the wrong things. I had no idea what the right things were, but when nobody said anything in response, Mom just kept on talking.

". . . and then I was missing my stupid phone charger and my phone was dead, and suddenly Jim called my mother's phone out of the blue to say he had flown in and was at the airport and needed a ride. So we all went to go get him and then we got home and Rebecca *still* wasn't there. But we found your note, so we came as fast as we could. We came . . . *here*." Mom stopped talking again and looked around the room. When she spoke again, her voice was almost a whisper. "I know it all sounds insane and disorganized, but . . . she doesn't need to be *here*."

"No," said Officer Johnson in his warm, calm, strong voice. "I guess maybe she doesn't."

Then Mom stopped giving her manic speech and

turned to look at me instead, straight at me. "I'm so sorry, Rebecca," she said. "I'm so sorry. I was angry. I was angrier than I had a right to be."

It was funny when she said that. It was funny she was still thinking about it. With everything that had happened to me, I'd pretty much forgotten about the fight.

"It doesn't matter now," I said as I squeezed my dad's hand. Mom tried to smile. She looked very alone, standing at the counter, staring at me and Dad, clutching her purse tightly. She turned back around to Officer Johnson and asked, "Now what?"

"Well," he said, "Rebecca has quite a story to tell. She got herself locked in a basement today, but she says she doesn't want to press charges. Is that okay with the two of you? No charge, no file . . ." He raised his eyebrows at my mom, and then at my dad. "Easier on you, if you want my opinion."

"I guess so," Mom said. "I mean, I want to hear more about this, but for now, can I just take her home?" She turned to my dad. "Jim?"

Dad nodded. "Sure, I guess. As long as she's okay. We'll talk to Rebecca and be in touch."

Officer Johnson looked down at me. "She seems mostly okay," he said. "She's a good kid and she got lucky, but it isn't every day that cases like this end so well. Who knows what will happen if she runs off again?"

"I won't!" I blurted out.

"No, I don't think you will," he said, smiling.

I smiled back.

"You want my unsolicited advice?" he said to Mom. "Go home. Get some sleep. Work out your business. Talk to your kid. But for God's sake, charge your phone, lady!"

Then he said "Good night, Kim" to the DFCS lady, who'd just been sitting there all that time. He walked past us, back out to the parking lot. I couldn't help wondering if he always worked so late.

That left the three of us—Mom and Dad and me—to wave an awkward goodbye to Kim ourselves. We walked across the parking lot in the dark. We didn't say anything, just got into our old green car, which felt funny. It had been a long time since just the three of us had been in the same place at the same time. I climbed into the backseat beside the empty car seat.

Up front, Mom and Dad sat in silence. Mom started the car and pulled out onto the road. Nobody said anything, not even Mom.

After everything that had happened, why couldn't they talk? Why couldn't they be happy to be together? Dad had flown all this way to be here, with us, and Mom couldn't apologize for leaving? I realized that even though Dad was here now, they could still screw things up. They could have been through all this, been this miserable, and still . . .

I cleared my throat. "I have something to say."

Dad turned around and smiled at me. Mom glanced quickly over her shoulder, then looked back at the road. "Yes?"

"I just want to say that I'm sorry I stole the jacket. Also I'm sorry I ran away. I'm sorry I've been so bad lately."

"Jacket?" asked Dad. It was the first thing he'd said since we'd gotten into the car. "What jacket?"

"Oh, honey," said Mom with relief. "Let's just put this all behind us. Okay?"

"But," I continued as if they hadn't interrupted me, "*but* I need to go home."

Mom didn't respond.

Dad let out a huge breath.

"I *need* to go home," I said. "Right away. I'm not picking sides, and I don't care if you love each other. I'm not trying to force Mom to do anything, and if Dad wants to be silent and never get a job, I guess that's fine too. You can both be however you want. But I am a person and I have a home, a real home, and I deserve to be there. No matter what happens, I'm going home with Dad. It doesn't mean I love anyone more or less or anything. It only means I need to go home."

Then I sat back.

Mom stared at the lights of the other cars on the road in front of her and said, "I know."

She knew.

Then she talked, and this time I listened.

"I'm sorry, Rebecca," she said, clutching the steering wheel and keeping her eyes on the road. "I'm so, so sorry. I'm afraid I was very wrong to bring you here, like this." Her voice was even.

Dad was watching her intently, silently.

"It's okay," I said.

"No," Mom said. "It's not okay. It isn't. The thing is, I knew this would be rough on everyone." She paused. "I was ready for that. I thought that part out before I made my decision. I thought it out a little bit, anyway. Only I didn't have any idea just how wrong it was. To leave. I knew I was leaving him"—she jerked her head toward Dad, who was still just sitting there—"without *me*. I meant to do that. I wanted him to see what it felt like to be without *me*. I felt taken for granted, and I wanted to see what it felt like to be by myself, to be alone. But it wasn't fair to force *you* to be without *him,* and *him* to be without *you*. He's a good dad. I'd forgotten how much kids need their fathers. You'd think I would have realized, considering my own . . ."

"I just miss him a lot," I said with a sniffle. It was cold in the car.

"Well, tonight, when we didn't know where you were, before we knew what had happened, *I* found out what it felt like . . . not being able to get to you. I remembered what it was like to be run away *from*."

"I'm sorry I ran away," I said, wondering what exactly my mother had to remember. Wondering again why nobody ever talked about my grandfather.

"He's your dad, after all," she said. "He *always* will be. No matter what I do."

"Oh, Annie," Dad said.

Nobody said anything else for a bit, and I stared at the road, at the back of my silent father. I wondered what he was thinking. Mom switched on the radio.

Then, because sometimes crazy things happen, because the world is big and small and full of magic, or coincidence, the song came on. Our little car filled with that familiar voice, full of gravel and ache.

> *Got a wife and kids in Baltimore, Jack . . .*
> *I went out for a ride, and I never came back.*

I sat and listened to the words I knew by heart. We all did, each of us staring out at the dark night through three different windows.

> *Everybody needs a place to rest . . .*
> *Everybody wants to have a home . . .*
> *Don't make no difference what nobody says . . .*
> *Ain't nobody likes to be alone . . .*
> *Everybody's got a hungry heart.*
> *Everybody's got a hungry heart.*

Lay down your money and you play your part.
Everybody's got a hu-u-ungry heart . . .

I could only think how weird it was that my mom wasn't crying. All my life she'd been crying, and now, here we'd had this scary, confusing thing happen, and she hadn't shed a tear. She was as still and stonelike as Dad.

Then the song was over. I knew I didn't want this time, this honest, hard, strange time, to be over without asking what I needed to know. So I leaned forward between my parents, straining against my seat belt, and asked, "Will we . . . will we still be a family when we get home?"

It was Dad who answered for once. "We will *always* be a family, Becks. No matter what. No matter what anyone does."

There was a pause then, a long one.

It was a good answer. It was a nice answer, but it wasn't enough.

"But will we ever live together again? Like a real family?" I asked, this time a little louder. "Like before?"

Neither of them said a word.

"Dad?" I said. "Mom?"

And then I heard a sound. A sound I'd never heard before in my entire life. The hardest sound, the softest sound, the most awful sound I had ever *wanted* to hear. I heard quiet sobbing. Tears and shaking breath and then, louder, up-from-the-gut sounds like an animal makes when it's in pain. My dad was crying, out loud. He cried like Lew when he's having a meltdown. I wanted to climb up front and hug him. I reached out to touch the back of his head, and it only made him cry harder.

There was nothing for me to do.

When he was done crying, my dad laughed. A tiny laugh. "You know what's funny?" he said.

"No," said Mom. "I don't. Nothing feels funny tonight."

"Just," he said, "just that . . . I haven't listened to that song since you all left."

"Really?" I asked. I had a feeling I knew what was coming.

"Yeah," he said. "I lost my iPod . . . somewhere."

Lew was waiting for me when we got home. We all fell through the door, worn out from everything that had happened. Gran had fallen asleep in her rocker, but Lew was sitting on the living room floor, under his blanket, in his pajamas. I crawled under it with him, the part of me I could fit. It wasn't a very big blanket.

"Hi," I said. I kissed his head.

"Hi, Babecka," he said. He grabbed the crook of my elbow with his soft little hand and just held it. He leaned against me. We sat like that for a minute.

Then he said, "Daddy."

Just like that.

"Yeah," I said. "Daddy."

Chapter 23

The next morning, Gran took Lew out for a last special date at the coffee shop and the playground, while Mom and I moved around the house, packing and shoving things into suitcases and trash bags. Meanwhile, Dad lugged all our things out to the car, then played luggage geometry like he usually does before a trip. There was a lot to pack. It seemed like we were leaving with more than we'd brought.

As I folded shirts and fitted toothbrushes into plastic Baggies, I thought about how I hadn't known we were leaving Atlanta, so I hadn't said goodbye to anyone. We were leaving Atlanta the same way we'd left Baltimore, and that bothered me, because it made me realize that in a way, we were running away *again*. I knew I didn't have a lot of people who'd miss me in Atlanta, but there were people *I'd* kind of miss.

I wished I had a chance to tell Mr. Cook I'd liked his poems. I wished I could show Mrs. Hamill that I really did know all about mass and matter. I wished I could tell Megan that I thought she had pretty hair. I knew I'd miss Megan, and I thought maybe someday I'd come back to visit Gran, and we'd see each other again. Maybe I'd even email her from Baltimore. She could tell me if Coleman really did end up boycotting the holiday show.

Most of all, I'd miss Gran. I'd miss her a lot.

Later, when we were done packing, once everything was in the car, while Mom and Dad were out front staring at a map and arguing about whether to take I-81 or I-85, I went to the room that was finally beginning to feel like mine and stared at the bread box.

I picked it up. Then I walked through the empty house. I stopped to get a hammer from underneath the sink before heading down the steps and into the backyard.

In the middle of the lawn, I set the bread box down.

I raised the hammer above my head, pointed it at the gray sky, and kept it there a minute like that. My arm began to get tired. I felt the heaviness of that hammer in my hand, felt the weight of it in my arm, my shoulder. Gravity was ready to bring it crashing down on the thin metal box.

But I lowered my arm. I uncurled my fingers and dropped the hammer gently onto the grass at my feet. Instead of tearing that box apart, beating it to pieces, I sat down beside it, crisscross-applesauce, like a little kid, on the damp ground. I closed the door of the bread box, thought for a minute, and made a silent wish.

When I opened the door, there was a seagull!

I smiled, let the gull out, and closed the box again.

I made another wish and opened the door, then let *that* gull out into the yard. It joined the first.

I wished and wished and opened and closed the door, and gull after gull joined me in the yard. Some of them sat and some of them flew, and some of them found a place in the trees above my head, the trees that stretched out their bare branches into the wintry sky. I wished for a hundred gulls, or more. I lost count. I'm not even sure why I did it, but soon the air was full of *skrreeee!* Then I closed my eyes and tried to imagine I was already home, but the air smelled like Georgia and the dirt felt like clay. That was fine now. I stood up and walked back inside, through the kitchen, and straight to the car with my bread box.

Maybe if this were another story, I'd have put the box back where I found it in the attic. Put it back where it belonged. Or maybe I would have had the courage to rip it apart with that hammer in the yard—either because it was capable of doing bad things or because I thought I'd already gotten what I needed from it. I think I took that hammer into the yard with me because I figured that was how the story *should* end—with me giving up the magic.

But the thing is, this is *my* story, and I couldn't stand to leave it behind. Because there are still going to be times when I want to find something—something I've lost. Something that belongs to me. Maybe even something that's been mine all along.

So instead I left the seagulls behind me, and I left something else too, especially for Gran. A present. Because I knew she'd be sad when we left. I knew she'd miss me even more than I was going to miss her, and I didn't want her to think I was running away.

Right where the bread box had sat all those weeks on the desk, I left my locket, the locket Dad had given me. It was mine to give and I didn't need it anymore. Inside it I left a tiny note, a scrap of paper for only Gran to read. It just said *"To Gran. From Rebecca. With love."*

Somehow, leaving something behind made me feel better about taking the bread box home with me to Baltimore. Where I *knew* I belonged. In my old room. In my little row house. In my real life. Whatever that was going to be from here on out.

I know there are lots of things the bread box won't ever be able to do for me. I get that. Magic can't always fix things for you. Because some people *do* leave. Some people let go and forget. Some people rip things apart.

But you know what? Some people don't.

ACKNOWLEDGMENTS

Bigger than a Bread Box isn't autobiographical. My mother did not toss me in a car, and my dad was never unemployed. Also, sadly, I never found a magical bread box in an attic. But I did harvest a lot of childhood memories to write this book, and that process tore me up. I cried a lot. I dripped on my keyboard.

So to begin with I owe this book to my mom and dad. They were generous in allowing me to misremember their divorce for my own selfish purposes, and I can't thank them enough. Their permission was something I needed to have before I could dive into my own past, because it is nearly impossible, in a family, to tell where one person's story stops and another person's begins.

I owe a great debt, too, to my husband, who watched me wrestle with this book. He was supportive and patient, even as I was baring my teeth and trying to understand how a woman might reach the end of her rope. I'll say no more about that, except that I'm lucky to be married to such a man.

As well, I owe this book (as I owe all my books) to my agent, Tina Wexler, and my editor, Mallory Loehr, who did *not* laugh at me when I told them I was writing a "middle-grade book about Bruce Springsteen songs and seagulls and divorce and a magical bread box." Their encouragement of my insanity is remarkable.

I owe much to Ellice Lee, Kate Klimo, Chelsea Eberly, Naomi Kleinberg, Jason Gots, Alison Kolani, Elizabeth Zajac, Lisa Nadel, Nic Dufort, Sarah Nasif, and everyone else I work with at Random House. I owe a debt to the booksellers and librarians and teachers who do so much to get books into the hands of curious kids.

And I want to mention that a great number of people helped me by reading early drafts, or listening to me whine, or sharing their own stories. I fear I will miss someone if I try to name them all. But I must say that this would have been a different book if not for the friendship of Rachel Zucker, Natalie Blitt, Gwenda Bond, Emma Snyder, Marc Fitten, Patrick Brickell, Robyn Morgan, Kurtis Scaletta, Julianna Baggott, Kris Willing, Linda Parks, Paula Willey, Jennifer Laughran, Sonya Naumann, Pieta Brown, Terra McVoy, Deborah Wiles, Laurie Watel, and Alan Gratz.

Last, but not least, I owe this book to Baltimore—which will always be my home. It is the most beautiful city in the world to me, and I will never shake the seagulls from my hair. But I also owe this book to the ever-changing landscape of Atlanta—because although it will never be the city that shaped me, it's the city that's shaping my children . . . and that makes it home to me.

It's eerie how much LAUREL SNYDER has in common with Rebecca Shapiro. Both of them grew up listening to Bruce Springsteen. Both of them have separated parents. Both of them have a Jewish dad who used to drive a taxi. And both of them have lived in Baltimore and Atlanta. There are a few differences, though. For one thing, there was no such thing as an iPod when Laurel was twelve. And while Rebecca hasn't yet decided what she wants to do when she grows up, Laurel has definitely decided to be a writer. In fact, she has written several books, including *Up and Down the Scratchy Mountains, Any Which Wall,* and *Penny Dreadful.*